Her bare skin was silky soft

Will sought the release for the top of the dance outfit Renae wore, then gave up and dived for her waistband.

She laughed teasingly, and moved out of reach. "Wait a sec. I have to call in to work and let them know I'm going to be a little late."

Will raised an eyebrow. "A *little* late?"

He took her hand and pressed it against his pants, letting her feel the rock-hard arousal underneath the thin material. He watched her pupils grow large in her green eyes.

"Okay," she said slowly, "maybe a lot late."

He reached out and dipped a fingertip inside the top of her bra cup. "Maybe you should tell them you'll be out the whole day...."

He watched her swallow with some difficulty. "The whole day?" A slow, sultry smile spread across her lips. "You really are looking to repeat the other night, then."

He grinned wickedly. "And then some..."

Dear Reader,

In the first two SLEEPING WITH SECRETS titles, *Forbidden* and *Indecent,* we willingly passed into the shadowy side of sex and love with our characters, but in this book... Well, not even we were prepared for the traditional male-female roles Will and Renae naughtily blurred....

In *Wicked,* E.R. surgeon Will Sexton doesn't know what hit him when Renae Truesdale—the sexy neighbor he's indulged in wicked fantasies about for the past three months—decides to test his playboy ways. But when hot, sticky sex evolves into so much more, can Will handle Renae's extensive sexual résumé?

We hope you find Will and Renae's journey to sexual enlightenment and love everlasting as provocative as we did. We'd love to hear what you think. Write to us at P.O. Box 12271, Toledo, Ohio 43612, or at karayianni@aol.com, and visit us on the Web at www.BlazeAuthors.com and www.ToriCarrington.com.

Here's wishing you love and hot, memorable reading!

Lori & Tony Karayianni
aka Tori Carrington

Books by Tori Carrington

WICKED

Tori Carrington

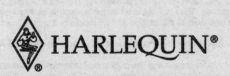

HARLEQUIN®

TORONTO • NEW YORK • LONDON
AMSTERDAM • PARIS • SYDNEY • HAMBURG
STOCKHOLM • ATHENS • TOKYO • MILAN • MADRID
PRAGUE • WARSAW • BUDAPEST • AUCKLAND

We dedicate this book to Cissy Hartley, Sara Reyes,
Celeste Faurie, Debra Evans, Helena Beasley, Lee Hyatt,
Janice Bennett, Kathy Boswell and the entire gang at
Writerspace.com. Thank you for providing a warm and
wonderful forum that lets us be fans as well as authors.
See y'all in the chatroom!

ISBN 0-373-79149-6

WICKED

Copyright © 2004 by Lori and Tony Karayianni.

1

SIZE DOES MATTER.

Emergency Room Surgeon Will Sexton had always believed that to be the case. But being British, he liked that Americans actually understood that. There was no such thing as the size of the ship doesn't matter, it's the motion of the ocean. As he dragged himself home after twelve straight hours on duty at St. Vincent Mercy Medical Center in Toledo, in a mammoth SUV that could comfortably hold three families, he brightened at the thought that once inside his large condo, set back on a large piece of land, he could collapse on his large king-size bed. It all added up to a vastness he'd never come across anywhere in working-class Southwark, England, just south of the Thames outside London.

Will parked his car in the large lot, which was designed to hold other large cars and was never without a free space, and climbed out onto the hot asphalt. The hazy August sun was beginning to peek over the horizon as he made his way down the long walk that led to his large condo and thus to his large bed. Okay, so yes, occasionally he did miss his bangers and mash. And it very rarely got this hot in jolly old England. But ever since skipping over the pond that was the Atlantic in order to earn his degree at the Medical College of Ohio nine years ago, he hadn't been back home for more than a week's stay. Fact was he'd grown comfortable, liked it here with the Yanks. Not only was everything around him bigger, but the citizens themselves seemed to think bigger. Well, maybe not all of them, but if one were inclined to take his life into his own hands, one could make a run of it here a lot easier than he could make it back home. Work hard, and you were rewarded well. Seemed like a good, solid philosophy to him.

And if William Charles Sexton, middle son of Dorothy and Simon Sexton, housewife and meat factory worker, respectively, had done anything throughout his life, it was work hard.

And he'd been well rewarded.

Will hiked his duffel a little higher on his shoulder. Still, somehow he thought he'd never get used to the hot summer weather here in the midwestern U.S. Heat and lots of it seemed to be the name of the game as of late. Actually that applied both literally and figuratively when it came to his life.

His good, if exhausted, mood took an immediate nosedive at the reminder.

Five months. That's how long he'd gone without sex. And not because of a size issue, thank you very much. Rather he'd been dating senior resident Janet Nealon for the past five months. And it was just his luck that Janet had decided the month before they'd started going out that she was going to wait for her wedding night before she had sex again.

Again.

Will hiked his duffel up again and scowled.

"Ah, one of those born-again virgin types."

He recalled his best mate Colin's words when Will had complained about the state of his sex life a few months back.

"Those are the worst kinds."

Will had made the mistake of asking him how so.

"Well, because you know they've given it up—they're just not giving it up to you."

Will eyed the six-unit building that held his apartment, his gaze immediately drawn to the condo on the third floor, directly above his. Of course, it didn't help that the female neighbors in 3B had cast themselves in starring roles in his growing sexual fantasies. It seemed not a night went by that he didn't think of the two hot lesbians in bed together, sweaty and naked. Crikey, he'd had to change his sheets just last week after a particularly steamy dream in which both women had taken a great deal of pleasure from working on *him*.

Of course, he knew that if Janet finally gave in, his fantasy life would vanish. Well, maybe not disappear entirely—after all, the two women fantasy was a popular one among men his age and he didn't see that changing anytime soon—but at least he wouldn't have to rely on those same fantasies to give him the physical release he needed.

And he wasn't going to take things "in hand" himself, as Colin had suggested he do.

The problem was he was getting nowhere fast with Janet. The night before last, before she'd left for a ten-day medical seminar in L.A., he'd pulled out all the stops during their hot and heavy petting session, taking great satisfaction in bringing her to orgasm. But when he'd convinced himself she was going to return the favor with some primo, long overdue sex, she'd buttoned up her blouse, kissed him lightly on the mouth, then thanked him before handing him his coat, so to speak.

Will's teeth had been set so tightly together his jaw had hurt.

It was a good thing Janet seemed to meet some internal criteria that he'd set up long ago with her fresh good looks and her bubbly disposition. Still, he didn't know how long he could stand it.

He pulled the door to the building open and froze.

Considering the sad state of affairs, this would happen to him, only to him.

On the stairwell coming down stood the number one billed star of his fantasies from 3B, Renae Truesdale. Will squinted at her. And if he wasn't mistaken, she was wearing what looked like…what appeared to be… He swallowed hard. She was wearing a bloody belly-dancer outfit. At eight o'clock in the morning.

Oh, he really didn't know how long he was going to be able to stand it….

RENAE TRUESDALE KNEW two things for sure: that sexy doctor Will Sexton from 2B thought she was hot, and that sexy doctor Will Sexton thought she was a lesbian.

She slowed her steps on the staircase from her third-floor condo, the gold disks that made up her top and the low waist of her belly-dancer costume giving an enticing jingle. Of course, it went without saying that she'd had the hots for the doc since she'd moved in six months ago. Who wouldn't, what with all that wavy, slightly disheveled light brown hair, bedroom-blue eyes and lopsided naughty grin? Oh, and then there was that irresistible British accent and his hesitant mannerisms that made it seem that he was thinking bad, bad thoughts every time she ran into him.

And now was no exception.

Of course, she wasn't a lesbian. Her roommate, Tabitha, was, but she wasn't. But she had come to enjoy playing up Will's misperception to delicious perfection. There were few things more satisfying than watching a man as attractive as he was treading foreign waters. No matter how acceptable the alternative lifestyle was becoming on television and in the media, the simple truth was that not very many people actually knew someone gay or lesbian, much less could call one a friend.

From personal experience Renae also knew that certain men were turned on by the thought of two attractive women living together, whether or not they were homosexual. Will, with his throat clearing and hot gazes, definitely fell into that category.

"'Morning, Will,'' she said, purposely swaying her hips as she descended the remainder of the stairs with suggestive jingles and shakes until she stood in front of him.

She watched a swallow make its way down his throat, past his Adam's apple even as his gaze plastered to her breasts, then lower to her bare stomach and the red crystal navel ring she wore.

"Um, yes. 'Morning.''

At some point she really should put the poor guy out of his misery and tell him that she wasn't a lesbian. Her smile widened. But not this morning.

Not when he looked about a breath away from climaxing on the spot.

As the only daughter of a stripper, she'd learned long ago that it wasn't so much what you said that mattered, but the time you chose to say it. No one had to know of her challenging upbringing unless and until she decided to share it with them. The same went with her friendship with Tabitha. She and Tabby had been best friends ever since high school, well before Tabitha's coming out of the closet, and when her friend had said she'd needed help with the condo payments six months ago when she'd been laid off, Renae hadn't hesitated to move in and share the financial burden, no matter what everyone thought.

Especially no matter what handsome doc Will Sexton and countless others believed.

He cleared his throat again and gestured toward her apparel, the back of his hand nearly grazing the tips of her breasts. "Um, going to work, are we?"

Renae couldn't help a small laugh. He looked so uncomfortable, so damn sexy. "Yes, I am."

Oh, she knew full well that he had no idea what "work" for her constituted. Seeing what she was wearing at 8:00 a.m. on a Saturday morning, she could only guess what he was thinking. And shoot her if she was wrong, but she was pretty sure his idea didn't include the Women Only shop where she did retail work along with teaching belly-dancing classes. While she normally didn't wear her costume to work, she'd been running late this morning and had discovered that she hadn't any acceptable clean clothes to wear. So she'd improvised.

Besides, she'd reasoned, who was going to see her that early on a Saturday morning?

She'd forgotten that was the time Will usually came home.

She pulled the side of her bottom lip into her mouth. Then again, maybe she hadn't forgotten at all.

"Do you, um, you know, give private shows?" he asked.

Renae raised her brows. While she normally enjoyed teasing Will, this was the first time he'd come out and said something so blatantly and directly sexual to her. She'd figured it was because he couldn't quite wrap his mind around the whole lesbian angle. That he was coming on to her now marked a change of sorts. A change she wouldn't mind encouraging.

"Mmm," she said evasively, a shiver running over her exposed skin at his continued visual interest in her and her costume. "It all depends on who wants the performance."

Something about the way he stood gave her the distinct impression that he was about to grab his wallet out of his back pocket and offer her any amount she wanted to perform for him.

Little did he know she'd do it free of charge.

"I see," he said, clearing his throat again.

Renae gave a wicked shimmy. "Don't you just love the costume?"

His gaze flew to hers. "Love...yes. I daresay it is an intriguing bit of apparel." He gestured again, his hand brushing against her breasts this time before he quickly drew it back. "There do seem to be parts of it missing though."

"Do you think?"

She swayed her hips, the metal disks clinking together again, drawing his gaze there.

While Renae didn't fool herself into thinking she was a perfect female specimen, she did know she was attractive, despite her shorter stature and her fuller curves. The ample size of her breasts alone was known to stretch a few necks. And giving belly-dancing classes over the past four months had honed the muscles of her stomach until they were defined, firm and supple. Her skin was tanned warm gold from the swims she took in the community pool every morning and afternoon when she knocked off of work.

Will's quiet chuckle surprised her.

"You're a tease, do you know that, Miss Truesdale?"

She considered him leisurely, suggestively. "Who said I was teasing, Dr. Sexton?"

His blue eyes darkened as he looked at her, plunging them both farther into uncharted territory.

Renae blinked, caught off guard by the rush of hormones through her system. What had been harmless flirting before had just moved into more serious, more sensual terrain. And, she was surprised to find, she wanted to explore it. If just for a little while.

And Will appeared equally willing. "Then what is it you would call what you do every time our paths cross?"

"Oh, I don't know," she said ambiguously. "Issuing you an invitation?"

"An invitation?" he echoed.

"Mmm-hmm." She stepped closer, smoothing down the collar of his crisp white shirt, the sleeves of which were rolled up to reveal his strong, hair-covered forearms. She'd meant to put him on alert, but found her own palms sensitized as she stroked the Egyptian broadcloth, feeling the heat of his body just below the material.

"An invitation to what, might I ask?"

She stepped closer, increasingly aware that she wasn't only arousing Will, she was arousing herself. Her nipples tingled in sweet anticipation, her stomach tightened, and her thighs squeezed slightly together. "What do you think?"

Her hips skimmed against his, and she instantly detected his very obvious physical reaction to her come-on. Oh boy. Suddenly she was having just as much difficulty swallowing as he was.

Who would have thought? While she'd always gotten a little thrill at flirting with Will, she'd never seriously considered pursuing anything with him. But as she stood there, well aware of the signals he was giving off, the signals her own body was sending her, she realized they'd reached a fork in the road. She had one of two choices: either laugh off the current sexual tension radiating from them both and walk away, or kiss him and let nature take its course.

Funny, but she didn't seem to be in a hurry to make either decision. Instead she allowed her gaze to drop leisurely to his mouth. His lips were so well defined. So sexy. So naughty. And she had little doubt he'd know what to do with them.

Liquid awareness swirled in her stomach then gathered at the center of her sex. She shivered slightly in response. How long had it been since she'd had sex? Gone out on a date, even? Too long, her body instantly responded. At least eight or so months. And even then the experience hadn't been anything to remember.

"You, um, should probably get going," Will said quietly.

Even as he said the words, Renae got the distinct impression that he didn't want her to go anywhere but up to his condo with him.

"Otherwise, you might be late," he continued.

Renae recognized the sexual tension that seemed to emanate from him and wind around her. She decided she liked the feeling. Liked knowing that Will wanted her but appeared to have his own reasons for not laying claim to her. Reasons that went beyond his misperception of her relationship with her roommate.

"Mmm," she finally agreed. "Yes, I probably should be going."

She said the words even as she knew she wasn't going anywhere.

DAMN IT ALL TO HELL, he was going to kiss her.

Will looked down into Renae's provocative face, suffering a need so consuming, so overwhelming it loomed outside anything he'd experienced before. Oh, he was a normal male with normal male urges. But considering what he knew about the woman looking up at him like the answer to his sexual prayers, the only thing he should be doing was heading for the door.

Instead he said, ''What would you do right now if I kissed you?''

Her full, luscious lips curved slightly upward in a sexy smile. ''Oh, I don't know. Kiss you back?''

That was all the answer Will needed. He curved his hands around her gloriously bare back and hauled her to him, noisy costume and all, not stopping until he'd molded her mouth to his.

Damn. He'd been hoping that her lips would be dry, her skill lacking. But kissing Renae Truesdale was nothing short of sweet heaven. Squared.

Or, rather, burning, seductive hell. Because surely that's where he was heading by kissing a woman who was definitely not Janet. A woman who led her life differently from the majority of society.

A woman who was making him not care a lick about any of it with every delectable flick of her tongue.

Will moved his hands against her back, growing all too aware of the softness of her skin, the suppleness of her warm flesh. Heavy breathing filled his ears and with a start he realized it was his own.

He groaned and caught her pert bottom in his palms, crowding her even tighter against his almost painful arousal. How easy it would be to carry her up the flight of steps to his condo. Lay her across his unmade king-size bed. Act out every last wicked fantasy he'd had about her ever since she'd moved in.

But to do so would be to tempt fate in a way he wasn't sure he should just then.

Unfortunately he wasn't having much luck convincing his hormone-ravaged body that it should care.

Renae's fingers had pulled his shirt from his trousers and were even now flattening against the taut skin of his stomach, her moves bold and mesmerizing. She slid her touch lower and cupped the length of him in her hand.

Will's answering shudder was so all encompassing that he feared if she suggested they do the deed right then, right there, he would be helpless to stop himself from pressing her against the wall of mailboxes and curving her legs around his waist.

The hand disappeared from the front of his trousers at the same time her mouth moved from his.

Will blinked at the sexy vixen, his brain little more than scattered gray matter turned to lustful mush.

"Well, I'd better get going," Renae said, her color high, the pitch of her raspy voice even higher.

He found himself nodding stupidly, his mind knowing she was right but his body screaming otherwise. "Yes, you'd better."

She smiled, skimming her luscious body against

his in order to gain access to the outer door. It was all Will could do to stop himself from collapsing against the wall of mailboxes. Thankfully he was still standing upright when she turned toward him.

"That was definitely interesting," she said, as if surprised and pleased at the events of the past few moments.

"Interesting…yes. That it was," he agreed.

And Will had the feeling that things were only going to get a lot more interesting from there.

RENAE LOVED WORKING at Women Only. The shop that sat on the Ohio-Michigan border was more than a job to her that provided a check at the end of the week. Ever since owner Ginger Wasserman had opened the place and hired her on the spot five years ago, she'd felt invested in the shop's success. Responsible for making the clientele happy. Dedicated not only to coming up with new ideas for services and supplies women might be interested in, but to seeing them through.

That was why it seemed strange that the shop was the last thing on her mind when she arrived there fifteen minutes after her intimate encounter with Will Sexton next to the mailboxes.

''Boy, you must really be looking forward to this class.''

Renae blinked Lucky Clayborn's pretty face into focus. More than her co-worker, she and Lucky shared similar pasts that had aided in their growing close over the past two months. And now that Lucky was opening up a satellite Women Only shop downtown, Renae saw more of her than ever. Which made coming to work doubly enjoyable.

''The costume,'' Lucky said by way of an explanation.

Renae stared down at the belly-dancer outfit she wore, almost surprised to discover she still had it on.

It had been a long time since a guy had driven her to the point of distraction.

Longer still since one had made her forget what she was wearing.

Very interesting, indeed.

''Your class awaits,'' Lucky said, motioning toward the curtained-off room to the right.

What had once begun as a traditional one-showroom retail shop had slowly expanded to take up four units in the strip mall that had once been Strip Joint Central. While a couple of men's clubs remained, Women Only was quickly growing to crowd them out and the area was becoming better known for catering to the positive needs of women rather than the baser needs of men.

To the left of the showroom were the cushy massage rooms and a comfortable class area designed to look like a large, inviting sitting room where everything, from how to give a blow-his-mind blow job to educating women on their G-spot, was discussed. To the right was the open studio room lined with mirrors where Renae and others taught belly dancing and, yes, even the art of stripping. But rather than for dollars, they taught them the skills to perform in private for their mates.

"Renae?" Lucky moved her hand in front of her eyes. "Are you all right?"

She considered the way her blood still thrummed through her veins, and the dampness of her thighs, and smiled. Oh, yes. Everything was more than all right. It was great.

"Fine. I'm just fine. Have you seen Ginger?"

Lucky wrote something down on a pad she held, seeming more than a little distracted herself. Which was normal, Renae thought. If she had a guy like Colin McKenna waiting at home for her every day, she'd spend the rest of her life with her head in the clouds.

"She was in and out already. Said she might be back after lunch." Lucky looked at her. "Did you want something in particular? You could always call her cell."

Renae made a face as she adjusted the top of her costume. What she had to discuss with Ginger couldn't be done over the phone. And she didn't want to make an appointment, either. Because to do so would indicate something was on her mind.

No, she wanted to catch Ginger when she had a free moment.

"No. I just wanted to ask her about some new stock, that's all," Renae fudged.

"Hmm." Lucky didn't appear to believe her. Which was odd, because there was no real reason why her friend should think her motives were other than what she professed. Were they that tuned in to each other?

She heard music from the other room and looked in that direction.

"The natives are getting restless. I'd better get in there."

She moved toward the curtained-off area, then paused at the door. "By the way, what do you know about Colin's friend Will?"

Lucky's pen stopped moving where she'd returned to writing something on her clipboard. "That he's a doctor."

"Very funny. I meant what specifically?"

Lucky squinted at her and smiled. "Like what is his favorite color?"

Renae gave her an eye roll. "As in is he seeing anybody?"

Lucky's eyes widened. "Oh." She put the clipboard down on the counter as the sound of Middle Eastern music grew louder in the other room. "I think he's dating a resident at the hospital."

Damn.

Of course, it was just her luck that the instant the

dynamic between her and the sexy doc changed, he'd already be involved with somebody.

Then again, she wasn't looking for involvement with him. She was looking for sex.

But she also didn't relish the idea of being the other woman, no matter how briefly.

Well, first things first, she had to decide if she really wanted more of those fireworks that had shot off between them that morning.

She blinked to find Lucky still staring at her. "What happened?" she asked.

Renae merely grinned. "Nothing. And everything. Remind me to tell you later."

She stepped into the room and drew the curtain closed behind her, ignoring Lucky's, "You can bet I will!"

THE BALCONY DOORS and heavy white vertical blinds were drawn tightly against the late-morning sun, casting the room in shadow, nothing but the ticktock of the clock his mother had sent him from England last Christmas and the central air-conditioning unit breaking the silence. At this time on a Saturday the complex was quiet, and now was no exception. Will knew from experience that the usual weekly hubbub of grocery shopping and errand running had yet to begin, and those seeking the community pool had yet to rouse from sleep.

Still half asleep, he dragged his wrist across his damp brow wondering if he should turn down the temperature of the thermostat. But he was all too aware that the summer heat wasn't to blame for his sweaty condition. Rather Renae Truesdale and the naughty dream he'd just had about her was responsible.

He rolled over then groaned when he nearly permanently injured himself. Holding up the top sheet, he stared at his erection, a hard-on that could rival Big Ben.

"At ease," he muttered, letting the sheet settle back down.

This wasn't going to do at all. Five months of waking to pulsing hard-ons. Dreams filled with images of women he shouldn't be lusting after. Hell, he was plowing through his supply of sheets because no matter what chilly temperature he kept the room at, he woke up soaked with sweat. For a short time, vigorous tennis matches with his mate Colin worked out much of the frustration. But lately not even that was working.

Especially since Colin had called the brutal matches to an end a couple of weeks ago claiming Will's unrelieved frustration was making the games too intense. Worse, Colin had tried to hand him money to buy a little female company.

Five minutes, Colin had told him. That's all it would take.

But just as Will hadn't masturbated since he was twelve, he'd never paid for it. And he wasn't going to start now.

He stared at the face of his alarm clock, surprised to find that he'd managed a few hours rest and that the buzzer was about to go off to wake him for his lunch date with Colin. He switched off the alarm, tossed off the top sheet then headed for the shower, turning on the water full blast and as cold as he could stand it. He climbed inside and gritted his teeth, waiting for the punishing spray to weaken his erection. After a few long moments, he cracked his eyelids open to find that the water was having absolutely zero effect on Ben.

Well, Christ. What was he supposed to do? Walk around all day trying to hide a hard-on the size of a baseball bat?

Unable to take the cold water anymore, he adjusted the knobs until the spray warmed, then leaned his hands against the ceramic tile and took a deep breath. Damn Renae Truesdale and her wicked belly-dancer costume. He put his face into the spray, remembering the soft globes of her breasts, the sleek smoothness of her skin, the defined muscles of her abdomen. Then there was her kiss…

His erection twitched and he groaned. It wasn't

fair, being offered up a temptation of Renae's caliber while he lay in wait for the woman who was supposed to end up the love of his life. Then again, he'd learned pretty early on that life was anything but fair. After all, what was the difference between him and Prince Charles but for the legs they'd popped out from between? While his mother had been trying to rub the ever-present mud from his face, Charles had been photographed on the finest of thoroughbred horses in his chaps, mud everywhere but on his elite person.

But when all was said and done, he and Charles weren't really all that different, now, were they? After all, Chuck had ditched a perfectly good princess in order to shag a woman he hadn't been able to exorcise from his system.

And Will was obsessed with the idea of banging the hell out of Renae Truesdale when the only woman he should be wanting was presently on the other side of the country.

He grabbed the soap and lathered up his hands, thinking even as he did so that no amount of soap would be able to cleanse the mud from his mind.

''Face it, you're not going to get her out of your head until you sleep with her.''

That was another thing that life had taught him. That no matter how much you wanted a woman sexually, the instant you had her, it was a whole new ball game. He couldn't count the number of times he'd woken up to find himself staring at a woman whom he'd wanted within an inch of his life the night before but whom he wanted nothing more than to run from the next morning. That's why he'd decided five months ago that in the future he would conduct his relationships with his head rather than with his Johnson.

Or in this case his Ben.

He stared down at the traitorous body part that was just begging to be touched. The problem was, it didn't want his attention. Rather it was more in-terested in seeing if the oral talent Renae had dem-onstrated with her kissing extended to oral sex. He ran his soapy hands over his stomach and arms, then lathered up again. He reached for his rock-hard arousal at the same time he imagined Renae's dec-adent mouth closing over the tip…and he came with the power of a twelve-year-old experiencing his first orgasm.

Oh…oh…oh.

When the spasms finally subsided, Will instantly released his erection and stared down at it with all the disgust of a man at war. This was not happen-ing. He had not just masturbated. He'd merely been washing himself and…well, Ben had taken over from there.

"You and me," Will said to the faithless organ

that even now seemed to be grinning at him in sated bliss. "We have to have a chat. A nice long one."

And not once, he decided, would the name of Renae Truesdale come up.

"YOU LOOK LIKE HELL."

Just what Will needed to be told in that moment.

He stared at Colin McKenna across the table from him even as he took a deep slug of a cold draught of beer. Harry's Bar was their usual hangout of late. It was where, if he remembered correctly, he'd met Colin's friend Lucky Clayborn for the first time. Well, right before she was fired as a waitress from the bar, became a patient of one of Colin's colleagues, then became the love of Colin's life.

"Right-o," he commented dryly. "Thanks for that astute observation, friend."

Colin chuckled and pushed aside the menu neither of them needed. "Dare I ask what's behind this morning's scowl? Or is it the same battle that's been raging for the past five months?"

"Same old battle," Will confirmed, downing half the ale and stretching his neck.

"Still not getting any from the new girlfriend?"

Will waved him away as he made room for the waitress to put down his fish-and-chips. Harry's was the only restaurant that came close to offering up something akin to what he'd grown up on at home. Fast food British-style. "No, it's not that."

Colin raised his brows. "So you are getting some?"

Will scowled. "No, no. Unfortunately."

"Then what is it if it's not that?"

Will tried to pick up a piece of fish, found it too hot, and shook his fingers to cool them. "It's just that…well, since my sex life is not quite up to par as of late, my fantasy life has geared up to take up the slack."

"Ah. The lesbians upstairs." Colin nodded.

"Actually, it's not both of them, but just one, as luck would have it." He chewed thoughtfully on a chip. "I had the most delicious encounter with Miss Renae Truesdale in the hall next to the mailboxes this morning."

Colin hesitated where he had just picked up his own chicken burger. "Define 'encounter.'"

"Oh, nothing out of the ordinary, mind you. Just some harmless flirting." The fish was finally cool enough to eat and he bit into it. "Oh, and the most phenomenal kiss," he said around a full mouth.

"You kissed her? Who initiated it?"

Will thought about it a minute. "I don't know. It was more of a mutual thing, I guess."

Colin's grin was altogether too self-satisfying for

Will. "I thought lesbians were considered lesbians because they weren't interested in men."

Will made a face and dragged his napkin across his chin. "Yes, well, maybe she's one of those new-fangled lesbians. You know, bisexual instead of homosexual."

He supposed he found the fact that Renae had kissed him a bit odd himself. While she'd played a starring role in his fantasy life, given her sexual status, he'd had no idea that she might be interested in him, no matter her playful flirting up until now.

"So what do you think I should do?" he asked.

"About what?"

The waitress supplied them with fresh draughts and made off with their empty glasses. "What do you mean 'about what'? What should I do about the intriguing Miss Truesdale, of course?"

"Oh, no." Colin put his burger down. "There's no way I'm getting involved in this. Lucky works with Renae, you know."

Will nodded, then shrugged. "Anyway, it's quite possibly a nonissue already. The instant she walked away this morning she probably realized her mistake."

"Mmm. Because it's easy to mistake you for a woman, you mean."

Will remembered the way she'd gripped his manhood. "No, I mean maybe she just…slipped or something.'' He shrugged as he downed another half a draught. ''At any rate, it should be relatively easy to avoid her.''

''If that's what you want to do.''

''Are you saying it isn't what I should want to do?''

''I didn't say anything of the kind.'' Colin opened the ketchup bottle and created a red puddle next to his perfectly good chips. ''But I am getting a little tired of hearing about your empty bed.''

Will squinted at him. ''So you think I should force the issue with Janet then?''

Colin took a deep breath then chuckled. ''I think you should do whatever it is you need to do, Will.''

''A whole lot of help you are.''

Yes, he thought. He'd avoid Renae. Shouldn't be too difficult. When he returned home from work in the mornings at the same time she normally left for work, he'd simply park in the far corner of the lot and wait until she left before going inside.

Yes. That should work out just fine.

And it wouldn't have to be for long. After all, Janet would be home in a little over a week's time.

''Now, how about we start up those tennis matches again?'' he asked Colin, who was already shaking his head.

3

OKAY, SO SHE WOULD avoid Will.

When Renae knocked off work, she was happy with her plan, and decided it should be easy to implement. After all, they kept very different schedules, and if it came down to it, she could always park in an adjacent lot on the other side of the apartment building to avoid running into him coming or going.

Truth was, she hadn't expected to feel so…attracted to Dr. Will Sexton that morning. Hadn't anticipated that the light, flirty tone that had always existed between them would dive into something more palpable and solid. When they'd kissed, no one had been more surprised than her. Pleasantly—no, blissfully—surprised, but surprised. After all, she wasn't in the market for a man just now, even for sex, no matter what her body was telling her—and what her growing budget for batteries to use with her private toys was telling her. It wasn't that she was antiman; it was that right now she needed to concentrate on her career. More specifically, she needed to convince Ginger Wasserman to let her buy into Women Only. Become a more solid part of the venture, and as a result take home a bigger piece of the pie.

Not that she wasn't being paid well for her work. She was. She shifted on the cracked white leather seat of her 1971 pink Cadillac Eldorado convertible. It was just that she wanted to feel more…connected somehow.

She was perfectly aware that she might not feel that way had it not been for Leah Westwood opening a Women Only shop in the west end of the city, then Lucky doing the same downtown. Had neither woman come into her and Ginger's lives, she would very likely still be operating the way she had for the past five years.

But they had and as a result she felt different. Wanted more. Her mind was functioning with more of an eye on the future, her future, and the bottom line.

Truth was, she wanted a place of her own to hang her hat at night. Sure, she might be able to afford a comfortable if small condo, or even a house, but she'd like something a little bigger, a little nicer, maybe. And while she was happy living with Tabitha, her roommate's girlfriend, Nina, made it clear she was very unhappy with the arrangement. Nina wanted Renae to move on, even though Nina had moved in three months ago while Renae had been there six.

She pulled her T-shirt away from her damp back, questioning the wisdom of driving with the top down when the August temperatures easily soared into the nineties at this time of day. Of course, Tabitha had no clue about the animosity that existed between the two women. And Renae didn't think it a good idea to point it out to her. Male-female, female-female, the gender of those involved didn't matter; a threat from the outside, from a friend or neighbor, perceived or otherwise, did.

She took a corner, the disks on the belly-dancer costume, wrapped in plastic in the back seat, jingling as she did so. She glanced down at the jeans, T-shirt and flip-flops she'd changed into at work, then back at the costume, a slow, easy smile turning up her mouth.

Will…

For a few sweet moments the tensions that littered her life melted away, leaving nothing in its wake but the memory of his skillful mouth and his hard, welcoming body.

Blame it on the heat, but she couldn't remember wanting a man as powerfully as she'd wanted Will that morning. Given the way she was raised, men and relationships had always been something to question rather than to surrender to. That's what she'd liked about Ginger Wasserman on the spot. Ginger understood her in a way that a Suzie Home-maker type never could.

And it's why she'd instantly understood that dark, lost look in Lucky Clayborn's eyes when she'd walked into the shop months back.

Renae pushed up her large, dark sunglasses on her nose and turned up the volume on the radio, hoping to edge the heavy thoughts out of her mind with a little rock 'n' roll. Heart's "Crazy on You" filled the humid air and she nudged the volume level up even farther.

Of course, it was just her luck that the tune would make her think of Dr. Will Sexton again.

She sighed. That's all right. She knew that a little time and effort and avoidance would put him right back where he belonged, which was solidly in flirt territory. Whenever her heart or her hormones threatened to lead her in the wrong direction—which, granted, wasn't often—she knew that as quickly as the emotions surfaced, they could as easily die away. And if she ever questioned the phi-losophy, she needed only to remember the pillow-shock syndrome that nearly every red-blooded human being had gone through at one time or an-other. Namely that moment when you opened your eyes the following morning to find the person who had seemed perfectly suitable and lust-worthy a few hours earlier had turned into the person you wouldn't be caught dead with on a deserted island overnight.

And experience had taught her that the sudden, unexpected change in her playful connection to Will bore all the earmarks of pillow-shock syndrome.

Great sex material one day.

The date from hell the next.

She smiled to herself as the radio station launched into another Heart tune, this one more befitting her mood: "Even It Up." Forgetting she hadn't meant to, she began turning into the regular parking lot at the building, then at the last minute swerved back into traffic, earning her irritated honks from the drivers behind her. She waved her apologies then swung around to the back lot and claimed the last open parking space. She glanced at the SUV to her right, thinking it looked an awful lot like Will's....

Then he climbed out.

ALL RIGHT THEN, some sort of higher power had it in for him.

That was Will's deduction as he stood next to his SUV and stared at Renae, her long, tangled sun-kissed hair, her clingy white T-shirt that did little to hide the lacy bra she wore underneath and her big, black glasses that made her look like the one-hundred-percent luscious, hot American woman that she was.

He flinched when the radio station she was tuned in to launched into the opening strains of the old The Guess Who song "American Woman" before she switched the ignition off and plunged them both into a shocked kind of silence.

"Come here often, do you?" he asked with a raised brow, accepting that avoiding her now was out of the question.

She gave him a leisurely once-over then pushed her sunglasses onto the top of her head, her smile decidedly decadent. "Funny, I parked over here to avoid you."

He chuckled at her refreshing honesty. "Ironically, I was doing the same thing."

The way he saw it, the only thing to do now would be to walk with her to their building. To give her a brief wave then take off would be so appallingly rude as to make him shudder. So he waited as she pushed a button that put the top up on the hideous pink contraption she called a car, gathered what he could see was the costume she'd been almost wearing that morning from the back seat, then joined him next to his SUV.

"I know why I want to avoid you," she said as they began walking together down the path that would take them to their building. "But why are you avoiding me?"

Will was amazed by the myriad emotions pulsing through his bloodstream caused by merely walking next to the woman. For one, he couldn't seem to keep his gaze off her pretty tanned face, even though it was currently devoid of makeup. And the way he kept eyeing her T-shirt and jeans, one would think he hadn't seen a woman dressed in that way before. But it was the fact that he was inordinately interested in her feet, wrapped in her hot-pink flip-flops, that was the cause for the most concern.

"Are your feet actually tanned?" he found himself asking.

Renae looked down, appearing as caught off guard by his inane question as he was. The problem was he'd never before really noticed a woman's feet and whether or not they were tanned. And it was more than just the neon-pink toenail polish she wore. There was just something wickedly attractive about her feet that made him fantasize about seeing them sticking out of a tub full of frothy bubbles…while she sat gloriously naked on top of him.

"Why yes, I guess they are," she finally responded, throwing him a sexy little smile. "And you're avoiding my question."

Will stiffened a bit. "Well, it's not that I'm avoiding your question, actually. It's just that…"

He couldn't help grinning. "It's just that I can't recall it."

"Why are you avoiding me?"

"Ah, yes. That question." Will eyed their building that seemed to loom outrageously far away. He felt the urge to pull at his collar, although he wasn't wearing a tie but rather a white open-throat polo shirt. And a pair of stonewashed jeans and sports shoes he couldn't wait to get out of.

What was the question again? Oh, yes. Why was he avoiding Renae?

"Well, you see," he said carefully, "there's this little issue of another woman that I'm seeing—"

"The resident."

He squinted at her although the sun was behind him. "You know about her?"

"Lucky filled me in."

"Ah, yes. Lucky. Colin's Lucky, I presume?"

Renae seemed interested in his mouth as he spoke. "One in the same."

"And she would have shared this information because…"

"I asked for it."

"I see."

Will shoved his hands deep into the front pockets of his jeans despite the abominable heat. Partly because he was filled with the almost irresistible urge to tuck a windblown strand of her dark blond hair back behind her ear. But mostly because he was afraid where the itchy appendage might roam from there. More specifically down the line of her intriguing back to her nicely rounded bottom, which might make it necessary for him to usher her straight into his condo and the bed therein.

But while he couldn't touch her, he could look at her. And what a feast for the eyes she provided, too.

He cleared his throat. "And your reason for wanting to avoid me?"

She smiled. "Oh, pretty much the same. The resident."

He chuckled softly at that one. "You're avoiding me because I'm dating someone else?"

"Mmm-hmm. Why do you sound so surprised?"

"Because that doesn't strike me as something you'd do."

The pathway wasn't disappearing under his feet at the quick rate he'd like it to. But the building was finally coming up. Thank God. He honestly didn't know how long he could withstand such a strong dose of temptation incarnate without succumbing to it.

"How so?" she asked.

He shrugged. "I don't know. You seem like the type that when she wants something, she takes it."

"Funny," she said for the second time in so many minutes. "You strike me as the same."

He looked at her. Really looked at her. At the appealing shape of her mouth. The openness of her attractive face. The wanton invitation right there in her creamy-green eyes and said, "Your place or mine?"

Without batting an eye she said, "Yours, definitely."

IF THE HUNGER RAGING through Renae's body had been for food, she would have devoured an entire buffet.

No sooner had the door to Will's condo closed behind them than they were going at it like a couple of sex-starved teenagers, all groping hands and wild hormones. Her plastic-protected costume dropped to the floor along with her purse even as Will yanked up the hem of her T-shirt and cupped her breasts.

"Ouch," she said when he squeezed a little too tightly.

"Sorry."

The pressure quickly turned pleasurable. Meanwhile, she tugged his shirt out of the waist of his jeans and flattened her palms against the rock-hard length of his abs. When she suddenly shifted her head to the right, she made solid contact with his nose.

"Ouch," he said.

"Sorry."

Quickly their clothes dropped away to the sound of zippers being undone and fabric seams being ripped. Renae couldn't seem to get enough of him. From his arms to his back to his hotly throbbing erection, her fingers moved, her blood surging through her veins, her breath coming in rapid gasps.

Finally his fingers found her heat, burrowing through her tight curls then coming to rest against her swollen folds. She shivered, so close to climax that she surprised even herself. She bit down on her bottom lip as he parted her engorged flesh then slid a finger up her dripping channel then drew it back out. She started trembling so badly she nearly couldn't hold herself upright.

Oh, yes. This was everything and more than she'd hoped—she'd feared—it would be with the sexy doc.

"The bedroom's this way," he said unnecessarily as he turned her while barely breaking the contact of their mouths, bumping her nose in much the same way she'd bumped his moments earlier. Walking backward was awkward at best, especially given the liquid consistency of her knees just then. She bumped into a couch—white leather—then nearly toppled over a plant stand—white lacquer—before her back hit the doorjamb that led to the bedroom beyond.

They fell to the bed in a jumble of elbows and knees. Renae's breath rushed from her lungs at the feel of Will's elbow in her stomach and he made a low sound of warning and she looked down to find her knee a millimeter away from not only ruining the moment, but the entire lifespan of Will's sex life.

"Hold on…a sec," she whispered, working her leg out from in between his and bending it instead around his thigh. Then she removed his elbow from her stomach and lay back, licking her lips in anticipation. "Now, where were we?"

She watched his blue eyes darken and heard an almost animal-like growl emit from his throat as he launched a fresh attack on her mouth. Renae curved up into him, relishing the rasp of his lightly hair-covered chest against her smooth breasts. It had been a long time since she'd felt so out of her mind with need that she burned from the inside out. And Will was the only one with enough hose to put out the fire.

She kissed him several times then drew away so she could look at where his erection was pressed against her lower belly. She swallowed hard. And oh what a hose it was, too.

"Condom," she whispered urgently, taking his impressive length in her hands and stroking him.

He shuddered. "In the drawer to your right. Yes, right there."

Renae pulled out a matchbook promoting a nearby bar, a pen, then found what she was looking for. She opened the foil package with her teeth then rolled the cool, lubricated latex down his length, hoping it wouldn't roll right back off because of his considerable girth. The scent of rubber and of hot arousal filled her senses as her fingers finally met with his scrotum. She gave the hair-covered globes a leisurely, explorative squeeze then spread her legs farther and positioned him against her waiting flesh.

Yes...oh, yes.

He bent down and kissed her and she restlessly moved against him, trying to force penetration even as his tongue swirled around in her mouth. She rubbed her breasts against his chest, reveling in the flames seeming to lick along her skin to join the inferno between her legs. Will pulled her right nipple deep into his mouth and she moaned, throwing her head back against the white comforter—was everything in his place white?—and jutting her hips up hungrily toward his.

"Please," she pleaded, seeking the connection he was slow in giving to her.

Finally he parted her slick flesh, positioned himself against her portal, then sank in to the hilt, filling her beyond capacity. Filling her beyond her wildest imagination.

And finishing before they had even begun.

4

SWEET GOD IN HEAVEN...

Will's body finally stopped twitching and convulsing and he froze above Renae feeling a mortification he had never encountered before in his life.

There was no playing off what had happened. No pretending that the instant he had entered her he'd climaxed as fast as a thirteen-year-old who'd paid for the pleasure. Even as he called on every ounce of willpower he possessed to prevent it from happening, Big Ben quickly turned into Little Willy.

And Renae was making movements for him to get off.

Will rolled to the side and lay on his back staring at the ceiling. "Well, that was certainly unfortunate now, wasn't it?"

He saw it as a good sign that she hadn't immediately gotten up, put on her clothes and left without a word. He heard her head turn against the bedding as she looked at him. "Anticlimactic would have been my choice of words."

He looked at her, unable to stop the grin that threatened. "Well, for one of us anyway."

She began getting up and he gently grasped her arm and held her in place.

"Sorry. Bad attempt at humor." He fought to catch the last of his breath. "Give me a moment, will you? I can't possibly let you leave after putting in the worst performance of my life." He swallowed hard. "God, I haven't come that quickly since…well, never." He looked at her. "At least not since I was six and first discovered my penis was capable of providing pleasure."

"Six?" she asked with a raised brow.

"Mmm. I was a young starter."

She rolled to her side and propped her head up on her hand. "And a quick finisher."

He chuckled. "Very funny."

She lightly shrugged her shoulders, causing her delectable breasts to bounce. "Until you prove differently, that's going to be my story."

"Your story?"

"Mmm-hmm. You'll go down in my personal sexual history as Quick Withdraw McGraw."

"Ouch."

"You're telling me."

Despite the humiliation that threatened, Will found her easy banter putting him at ease. "What would be the female equivalent to what just happened?'' he asked.

"Oh, I don't know," she said quietly. "My reading a newspaper while you went about your business."

"Now that would be downright rude."

"Do you see a newspaper anywhere?"

Will considered the shadows playing against his bedroom ceiling. He hadn't opened the vertical blinds from the morning and the room was dim and cool.

And the woman beside him was sexy and hot.

"Be a good bird and hand me another condom, won't you?"

Renae blinked at him, then down at his growing erection. She lay back and reached into the drawer to get another square packet. "Are you sure you want to subject yourself to this again?"

He took the condom from her. "I think the question is are you game for another round?"

"Seeing as I can barely remember—oh!"

Freshly resheathed, Will rolled quickly back on top of her, pinning her arms above her head and allowing his gaze to roam over her deliciously shapely body. He spread her thighs with his knees then positioned the tip of his fully throbbing arousal against her once again. This time when he filled her, he took his time about it, absorbing her every shiver and quake…and keeping his own control tightly in check.

Finally he was into her to the hilt and she moaned. He kissed her mouth then pressed his nose against hers. "What was that you were about to say?"

Renae restlessly licked her parched lips, her heart thudding hard in her chest, her womb contracting to the point that she believed she might be on the verge of climaxing.

Considering that moments before she'd firmly believed that pillow-shock syndrome had struck hours too soon, the rush of physical need that suffused her muscles, and the sensational chaos Will was so easily re-creating in her, was…well…shocking.

And oh so nice.

He began stroking her with his manhood in a way few men knew how to, expertly skimming the head of his erection against her G-spot then withdrawing before plunging in and tilting his hips to hit her pleasure spot head-on again. Oh, nice was so not the word for the way she was feeling. Orgasmic was closer to the mark. Out of her mind with pleasure would also fill the bill. She curved her hands around his tight posterior and squeezed, holding him deep inside her for a moment longer and grinding her pelvis against his, cherishing the friction of his hair against hers.

Oh, yes. That was so much closer to what she'd expected. She moaned as he stroked her again. In fact, it was quickly surpassing it.

His hips stilled and she cracked open her eyelids, afraid he might have bailed before her again. Instead she found he wasn't climaxing. Rather he was cupping her right breast then bending to run his tongue slowly along her distended nipple. Renae swallowed hard, unable to blink as she watched him swirl the tip of his tongue around and around then pull her nipple deep into his mouth, seeming to tug on some sort of invisible chord that linked her breasts to her throbbing sex. Without his having moved his hips she felt ridiculously on the verge of orgasm.

She stretched her neck and closed her eyes, trying to regain control. She wanted this to last. Wanted him to deliver on his promise to perform better the second time around.

She wanted to make the risk she'd taken by coming into his condo with him worth it.

He withdrew halfway then plunged almost roughly back in to the hilt. Renae's back came up off the bed and a long moan escaped her throat.

Then before she knew it he was rolling so he lay on his back, her on top.

Considering she'd been on the verge of climax, she wasn't sure she liked this change in position.

At least not until he thrust upward and chased all coherent thought from her mind.

Bracing herself against his shoulders, she tilted her hips forward, then back. Oh, yes. That was so, so good. Will's size practically guaranteed a girl a good time. Of course on the condition that he could actually maintain an erection. What good was a big member if you couldn't keep it that way? But despite his unpromising beginning, the sexy E.R. doc was delivering everything and more than she had spent all day imagining.

Her stomach began trembling and hot, liquid fire exploded through her body. She gripped his shoulders tightly and threw her head back, riding the exquisite waves crashing through her like a trained surfer. Only not even she was prepared for the length and the power of her orgasm. As her muscles began to calm, she tried to calm her surprise at her incredible reaction. After all, when she'd handed him the second condom, she'd been devoid of any expectation.

Now…

Well, now that she'd just experienced what could possibly be the best orgasm of her life, she didn't quite know how to respond.

"And?" Will asked, fondling her breasts.

Another shudder worked its way through her body and she smiled down at him.

"And that was definitely worth the risk of giving you a second chance."

Damn, he was sexy. His hair always had a kind of just-got-out-of-bed look about it, but now that it had really been tousled, he looked like the worst kind of devil, grinning up at her with his lopsided, British grin.

She began to roll off him.

He stayed her with his hands on her legs. "Where do you think you're going?"

She blinked at him. It was three in the afternoon and she hadn't been back to her apartment yet.

"Oh, Miss Truesdale, I'm nowhere near through with you."

She playfully widened her eyes. She'd been so enthralled by her own climax she hadn't noticed whether or not he'd come again. "Oh?"

"Mmm. I figure since we've gone this far, we might as well go all the way."

Renae found herself licking her lips in sweet anticipation. "Excuse me, but isn't all the way what we just did?"

"Uh-uh." He shook his head, his fingers drifting from her outer thighs so he could press the pads of his thumbs against the magic button between her legs.

Renae moaned.

"That was just the appetizer. And I fully plan for this to be at least a five-course meal."

Renae gasped when he lifted her from his hips then coaxed her in the other direction so she still sat astride him, but facing his feet.

"Be a good bird and get me another one of those condoms, won't you?"

Renae reached back and took out a handful of condoms. She let them rain down on his chest as she grinned in naked challenge. "Now make this bird sing."

HUMPH. Seemed ironic somehow that while he was having such a hard time getting one woman in his bed, he couldn't seem to get the other one out.

Will stood drinking an extra-large glass of orange juice from the doorway to his bedroom. It was past 6:00 a.m. Sunday morning and, a part of him told him, time for his bed partner to make a graceful departure. In the hopes of rousing Renae from the sleep of the dead, he'd already made about as much noise as he possibly could with absolutely no luck at all. Of course, his being halfhearted about actually wanting her to leave was something he preferred not to think about just then.

Instead he idly considered other ways he might go about chasing her from his condo even as he leisurely leaned against the jamb and took in her silhouette under the white top sheet. Damn, but she was beautiful. Most women didn't fare a fraction as well within a few hours of him bringing them back to his place. But Renae... Well, Renae looked somehow even sexier after the hours and hours of great sex they'd shared. Her dark blond long hair was tangled, sure, but rather than looking like a nest where bats might consider taking up residence, it appeared soft and appealing, framing her tanned face just so. And while she hadn't been wearing lipstick when he'd run into her in the parking lot yesterday, her lips still somehow managed to look seductively pink and wet, as if awaiting his kiss.

His gaze slid down her shapely body, which he knew was naked under the sheet. From the curve of her exposed arm, to the soft swell of material against her breasts, down to her curvy hip, he visually roamed. He glanced down at the front of his own shorts, surprised to find Big Ben chiming the hour once again.

He raised his brows. It had been a good long time since he'd spent so many unbroken hours having sex. And he couldn't recall the last time he'd still wanted a woman this much after having had her myriad ways over more than twelve hours.

He moved his half-empty glass from one hand to the other then knocked loudly on the open door.

Renae smiled, cooed, then turned in the other direction, completely oblivious to his attempts to wake her.

Which had been the case for the last hour.

Will couldn't resist stepping closer and peering over her shoulder at her completely contented expression.

Intriguing…

Especially when she blinked her eyes open, reminding him of how vividly green they were, and looked up at him. Her smile widened even farther as she rolled to her back and yawned. "Good morning," she said, her voice husky.

"Yes, um, good morning to you, as well." Will stiffened and absently rubbed his chin. "You weren't planning on moving in here, were you?"

Renae turned her head to stare at him.

"Because, you know, if you are, I'd have to set some ground rules. Like no sleeping later than me. And—"

She grabbed a belt loop on his cargo shorts and tugged him forward. "No fear there."

Will's first reaction was to ask why. Then he remembered that he wasn't supposed to want her in his apartment for reasons other than sex.

"Ah, yes, that's right," he said. "You already have a roommate."

He remembered the other woman who lived directly upstairs. She had some kind of cat name. Tabby or Spot or something like that.

Then again, she wasn't just a roommate, was she? She was Renae's live-in lover.

Somehow over the past fifteen hours he'd forgotten about that.

Intriguing, indeed.

He blinked at Renae's purely teasing smile. "Jealous?" she asked.

"Who me?" He pressed his lips together then shook his head. "No. Not in the slightest." He handed her his glass of orange juice then jabbed a thumb toward the ceiling. "But someone else might be."

She pushed up to a sitting position, causing the sheet to drape around her waist and baring her full and delectable breasts. Breasts that bore red patches from his considerable attentions the night before. He rubbed his freshly shaven chin and imagined himself slathering lotion all over her delicious skin.

"Are you talking about Tabitha?" she asked after she finished off the juice and handed him back the empty glass. He wasn't sure he liked the secretive smile she wore. Well, okay, he liked it—a little too much if you asked his opinion—he just didn't like that he didn't know what had caused it. "That's so not what our relationship is about."

He bit back his instant query for her to explain

what it was about, then reminded himself that he didn't want to know.

This...Renae...them...this was a one-shot deal. As soon as she walked out the door, she wasn't going to walk back through it again.

She lay back in the bed again and crossed her arms behind her head, her bare breasts jiggling in an all too enticing manner.

In order for that plan to work, however, he actually had to get her out the door.

She looked at him from head to foot. "You didn't have plans this morning, did you?"

Will found his tongue suddenly altogether too big for his mouth. "No. You?" he fairly croaked, unable to pry his gaze from the engorged tips of her breasts.

She slowly pulled the sheet from the rest of her body, offering up even more delectable vistas as she smiled at him wickedly. "Oh, I think I can come up with one or two."

Funny, but Will no longer wanted her to leave....

5

FOUR HOURS LATER Renae was in the kitchen of the condo she shared with Tabitha, washing the dishes that had been left in the sink—dishes she hadn't dirtied—and humming to herself. She was idly surprised that the tune she couldn't seem to shake was the Heart song "Crazy on You."

She smiled, recalling the near look of panic Will had worn after they'd wrapped up their last sack session and he'd gotten a look at the time. They'd been just a few hours short of spending an entire day in bed together. And he hadn't looked too pleased at that realization. In fact, he'd looked two breaths away from piling her clothes into her arms and shoving her through his door butt naked just to finally get rid of her. No matter that certain areas of his anatomy had other ideas.

The only reason she'd left at all was that they'd run out of condoms, both from his drawer and her purse.

And even now she was wondering if she had one or two stashed away somewhere in other purses.

She laughed at what Will's reaction might be if she showed up at his door holding the foil packets. He'd been surprised enough that she, a so-called lesbian, had carried condoms with her. He'd probably look adorably shocked initially. Then he'd likely yank her inside his apartment where they could put the rubbers to good use. After all, as Will himself had said when she'd been about to leave and found another in her purse, "A good condom is a terrible thing to waste."

"Now that's one look I haven't seen on your face for a good long time."

Renae glanced over her shoulder at Tabitha who was placing a shopping bag down on the glass-top kitchen table.

"What? The look of getting properly laid?"

Tabitha smiled at her as she unloaded the grocery bag. "Yes, that would be it."

Renae tried to control her smile and failed. She finished up the dishes and dried her hands.

"Anybody I know?" Tabitha asked. She finished emptying the bag and then folded it up and put it in the recycling bin in the pantry.

"Uh-huh."

Tabitha raised a brow as Renae helped her put the food items in the refrigerator and the cupboards. "May I ask who?" Tabitha took two cans of iced tea from the fridge, handed one to Renae, then they sat down across from each other in the wrought-iron chairs around the glass table.

''Sure.'' Renae pointed to the floor below them with her thumb.

''Disappointing?''

Renae realized she was giving the thumbs-down sign and laughed. ''No, silly. I'm referring to our downstairs neighbor.''

Tabitha nearly spewed her drink all over the glass tabletop. ''Oh, God, say it isn't so.''

Renae enjoyed her friend's reaction.

Truth was, both of them had gotten a kick out of teasing Dr. Will Sexton all through the summer. Had enjoyed putting on their skimpy bikinis and heading for the pool, making extra sure when they ran into him to fertilize his belief that they were lesbians and causing it to grow even further.

Of course, it wasn't the first time the two friends had done something of that nature. The two of them had quickly become close friends their freshman year at Start High School, and had remained friends since. They'd gone through Tabitha's hesitant coming out their junior year. But even before Tabitha had told her of her orientation, Renae had always guessed at her friend's sexual preferences. When they went to football games Renae always commented on the players' tight buns, while Tabitha had always been more interested in the cheerleaders. Not because she'd wanted to be one, but rather because she'd wanted to date one.

And ever since they'd both hit puberty, they'd been aware that whenever two hot women were together, men were wired to fantasize about them being together in a sexual sense. And they'd learned how to work the weakness to perfection. Beginning with their senior prom where they'd been each other's dates. Up until now with Will.

"You explained that we aren't lovers, of course," Tabitha asked now, jerking Renae out of her reverie.

"Of course not."

"And he still slept with you?"

"Oh boy did he ever."

Tabitha's frown barely detracted from her brunette beauty.

Of the two of them, Tab had always been the more attractive. The one guys went after, obviously with little success.

"Did he...has he..."

"What?" Renae asked, knowing exactly what her friend was thinking. "Did he ask me to give you a call and invite you over?" She shook her head. "Interestingly enough, he didn't."

"But you expected he might."

Renae tilted her head. "Yeah, I guess I did. But somewhere after the first five minutes I completely forgot and I think he did, too.'' She looked at her friend suggestively. ''Until this morning, anyway, when he asked if you might be jealous.''

Tabitha shook her head. ''One of these days you're going to get yourself into trouble.''

''Nah. I think I'm a little too smart for that.'' She looked around, peering into the hall and the living room beyond. ''Speaking of jealous partners, where's Nina?''

''Nina's not jealous.''

Renae laughed. ''Now look who's heading for trouble. Nina was born jealous.''

''She was not.'' Tabitha waved her away. ''Anyway, tell me more about Dr. Will. Will you be seeing him again?''

Renae twisted her can around and around on top of the table then wiped away the condensation. ''I don't know. Maybe.''

''So last night was purely about sex.''

''Oh, was it ever.''

''So you have no designs on him beyond that?''

''I don't think so. After all, he does have a girlfriend.''

''Well, that's interesting.'' Tabitha reached across the table and stopped her from fiddling with her can. ''You just be careful, you hear? You wouldn't be the first woman to mistake great sex for a relationship.''

"Mmm," Renae admitted. "And I think you would do well to listen to your own advice." She gave her friend a wink.

"What's that supposed to—"

"Tabby, I was waiting for you outside. I can't believe…" Nina's words trailed off when she spotted Renae and Tabitha sitting with their hands joined. "Oh. Hi, Renae."

She said the words with all the friendliness a snake might give a field mouse.

Renae returned the greeting with a little more warmth then patted Tabitha's hands before releasing them. "That's what that means."

"You slept with her."

Colin's words startled Will to the point that he missed his serve on point. When he tried to retrieve the bouncing tennis ball, he lost his grip on his racket.

"What?"

Colin pointed his own racket at him from across the court at the private club. Colin had insisted they play here, despite the perfectly good courts at Will's condominium complex. "You know perfectly well what I'm saying. That belly-dancing lesbian that lives upstairs from you. You've slept with her, haven't you?"

Will grimaced wondering if he was that transparent to everyone. Because if he was, then he was going to have one hell of a problem on his hands when Janet returned from California next weekend. "You couldn't be further from the truth," he lied, concentrating all his efforts on making a killer serve.

The ball went slightly out and he reached for another ball.

Colin squinted at him. "Come on, Will. The look on your face doesn't come from taking things in hand."

"So to speak."

"So to speak."

"And why wouldn't it?" He served again, happy this time just to get in bounds.

Colin easily returned it. "Because you wouldn't look like you've just been screwed within an inch of your life, that's why. You wouldn't be so relaxed, and grinning all the time. And I swore I heard you whistling when you walked up. Masturbation does not a whistler make."

The sound of a racket being dropped. Will returned the volley and glanced at the next court, which was occupied by a couple of hot young women. One must have overheard Colin and had dropped her racket midreturn. The two women looked at each other and laughed.

"Oh, bravo, Colin," Will said, putting some extra elbow into the next return and taking some satisfaction in Colin's having to hustle to hit it. "I think I recognize one of those girls from the hospital. That's all I need, for rumors like that one to start making the rounds. 'Willing Will, who's not afraid to take matters into his own hands.'"

Colin chuckled and didn't even try to get the next volley Will fired over the net.

"Point, game and match."

"Good." Colin gathered the errant tennis balls then met Will at the net where they shook hands. "I don't think I could have withstood another half-assed match. I think I liked you better when you were frustrated."

Another round of giggles from the next court.

"Will you stop," Will said under his breath. "Just think what Janet's reaction would be if word of this circled back to her."

Colin stared at him as they left the court. "You should be more concerned about what she'd think if she found out you banged your upstairs neighbor." His eyes widened. "You didn't sleep with both of them, did you?"

Will waved his hand. "No, no. Just the one."

Colin moved a couple of steps ahead of him and prodded him in the chest with his covered racket. "Aha! I knew it."

Will cringed, catching on to the mistake he'd made.

Colin moved to walk beside him. "So how was it?" he asked quietly.

"Do I enquire about what goes on between you and Lucky after the sun sets?"

"All the time."

"And do you tell me?"

"Never."

"Well, then."

"Yes, but Lucky and I are a couple. You and..."

"Yes," he confirmed, refusing to actually state Renae's name.

"Your experience was a one-nighter. Strictly sex. It doesn't count."

"How do you rationalize that?"

Colin stared at him a little too closely. "Unless it wasn't just about sex."

They'd reached the parking lot and Will opened the back of his SUV and tossed his racket inside along with his gym bag. "Of course it was just about the sex, man. What, have you gone daft in the head?"

Colin had parked next to him and loaded his own equipment. "Well, then, that marks last night as sharing material." He closed the back of his own SUV. "So how was it?"

Will stared at him long and hard, then grinned. "Great."

"I knew it!"

"More than great—it was incredible. I mean, I don't know if it's because I'd gone without for so long, but we went at it for a good twenty hours straight. Well, I mean, with time-out for catnaps and showers and the like."

Colin blinked at him, the humor wiped from his face. "Twenty hours?"

Will nodded, thinking he'd need a crowbar to pry the grin from his face. "Uh-huh. Twenty hours. And even then we stopped only because we ran out of bloody rubbers."

Colin didn't say anything.

And Will decided he didn't like the thoughtful expression he wore. "What? Oh, for Christ's sake, what are you thinking now?"

"Oh, I don't know. I'm thinking last night might not have been about just sex."

"Are you insane? Of course it was. Whatever else might it have been about?"

Colin continued staring at him for a long moment, then shook his head and walked toward the driver's side of his SUV. "You forget, I'm a couples counselor."

"Oh, God, here it comes." Will wiped his face on a towel he'd taken from his bag then threw it back into the truck and closed the door. "I knew I'd regret covering for you back in med school."

Colin chuckled. "It's just that in my professional opinion when a relationship is just about sex, any sexual encounters last no longer than a half hour—an hour max."

Will pointed at him over the hood of his car. "Those are the key words. 'In your experience.'"

"In my professional experience."

Will scowled as he opened his car door. "Yeah, well, who asked for your opinion, professional or otherwise? I don't recall doing it."

He looked over to find Colin grinning at him. "Harry's?" he asked.

Will was half tempted to tell him to bugger off. "Harry's," he said, then closed his door and started the engine, pointing his SUV in the direction of the sports bar a short distance away.

Not about sex.

What a ridiculous notion.

THE FOLLOWING MORNING Renae was still smiling.

And still hadn't gotten around to doing her laundry.

She closed and locked the condo door after herself then turned toward the stairs, trying to keep from making too much noise in her belly-dancer costume.

Well, at least she'd gotten some sleep. After Tabitha and Nina had gone out to the movies at around six last night, she'd curled up on her bed with the latest yummy Stephanie Plum offering and had immediately fallen asleep, not to awaken again until her alarm went off an hour ago at six.

She supposed her body had needed the rest considering the workout she'd given it at Will's place Saturday night. But still, it had been a long time since she'd needed more than eight hours.

She began descending the stairs, her gaze automatically going to the door of 2B and a grin the size of Ohio took hold of her face. Just thinking about what she and Will had done...

Wow.

Of course, she had no intention of seeing him again. Well, aside from running into him in the hall. Their repeating what had happened was not in the cards.

A little voice asked her why.

And she answered. First, there was no way in the world they could possibly better what had happened between them. That night...that night easily ranked up there with the best sex she'd ever had.

She gave a little shiver.

Second, there was the matter of Will's girlfriend. There was no mistaking that he was seriously involved or else he wouldn't have brought her up before they'd headed to his place. And if there was one thing Renae wasn't interested in, it was becoming the other woman. She'd never been that stupid and certainly wasn't about to start now, no matter how good the sex.

And the sex had been good, hadn't it?

She rounded the staircase and began heading down the last leg toward the door, then stopped, much as she had two mornings ago.

There just entering through the door was Will, looking at her in the same stunned way she was looking at him.

"Um, hi," she said, forcing herself to descend the remainder of the stairs and ignore the watery condition of her knees.

He didn't immediately respond and she knew a moment of disappointment. Oh, don't tell her this was going to turn into one of those awkward morning-afters. A twist on the pillow-shock syndrome, awkward morning-afters were worse, mostly because, when you suffered from PSS, neither of you cared what the other one thought—your mutual goal was only to get out the door quick.

But with AMA, one of the parties remembered the tryst favorably while the other ran as far as they could as fast as they could in the opposite direction.

"Um, hi, yourself," Will finally said.

Renae made a face. Definitely AMA. And Will was the one doing the running.

All right. That was okay. She could deal with that. It wasn't like she was looking to repeat what had happened between them the other night anyway.

She began to pass Will, trying to come up with something casual, light to say before diving for the door, when he finally lifted his gaze from the floor, skimmed her costume, then said with a grin that nearly made her cream herself, "What would you say if I requested a repeat of the other night…costume included?"

Renae suddenly had a hard time swallowing. "I'd ask you when and where."

Will stared at her mouth. "How about here and now."

Renae smiled. "Supplies?"

He held up a bag and shook it. "Replenished."

"Then I'd say lead the way."

6
_____

SOMEWHERE IN THE BACK of Will's mind he knew a moment of pause. A part of him that he didn't want to give voice to understood that he shouldn't be doing what he was doing. When he'd stopped at the pharmacy on the way home from the hospital that morning to stock up on condoms, he'd convinced himself that he'd been doing it because he and Janet might finally be knee deep in some sex when she returned from California at the end of the week.

But a wicked little voice told him he'd known what he'd been doing all along. That's why he'd sped home, hoping he wouldn't miss Renae when she left for work.

He unlocked his condo door and hustled her inside, liking the way the metal disks on her costume chimed with her every move. Liking the way she looked all soft and hot and sexy in the decadent clothes. And liking that he'd be getting her out of the garments as soon as humanly possible.

And if he doubted she felt the same, the thought

was banished when she launched herself into his arms, metal disks and all, kissing him as hungrily as if he were breakfast and she hadn't eaten for days.

The bare skin of her back was silky soft as he sought a release for the top, gave up then dove for the back of the waist.

She laughed and moved out of reach with a clang of disks. "Wait a sec. I have to call into the shop and let them know I'm going to be a little late."

Will raised a brow. "A little?"

He took her hand and pressed it against his rock-hard arousal through the thin material of his scrubs. He watched her pupils grow large in her green eyes.

"Okay," she said slowly, "a lot late."

He reached out and dipped a fingertip inside the top of her bra cup. "Tell them you'll be out the whole day."

He watched her swallow with some difficulty. "The whole day?" A slow, sultry smile spread across her lips. "You really are looking to repeat the other night, then."

He nodded. "And then some."

RENAE'S FINGERS trembled so badly it took three attempts for her to extract her cell phone from her purse. Will had worked her right breast up and out of the top of the costume and was even now pressing his tongue against her distended nipple.

She suppressed a moan and gave him a slight shove. "Give me a minute."

He made a show of looking at his watch. "I'll give you twenty seconds."

Renae pressed the button on her cell for her phone book and received the message that there were no entries.

She stared at the color display, pressed the phone book button again with the same result.

That's odd. She had no fewer than fifty entries in there, the one for the shop the most important.

Will began to advance on her and she backed away, laughing. "You'd better behave or I won't give you a show."

"A show?"

She wondered if all Brits were as sexily handsome as Will was. If they were, she'd have to arrange a visit to London posthaste. "Uh-uh."

She shut off the wireless phone, then powered it back up, only to receive the same message that there were no entries in her phone book.

That was strange....

Will pulled off his green scrub top, revealing every inch of his honed and toned arms and stomach. Renae's mouth watered and for the life of her she couldn't recall the number for the shop.

Finally she was able to enter it, and then she was shutting off the cell and bunching her fingers in Will's hair. He was down on his knees in front of her, his face buried against her bare stomach.

"I love these belly ring things," he said, dipping the tip of his tongue inside her navel then through the thin ring that bore a red stone.

A shiver washed over Renae's body, the air-conditioning vent above her partially to blame.

Will's hot and wet attentions more to blame.

"Do you want me to give you a private demonstration or not?" she whispered.

"Hmm. Definitely yes."

"Do you have music?"

He blinked at her as if she'd asked him if he had lobster in the fridge.

"Something Greek would be nice. Or Middle Eastern."

Will seemed cemented to the spot on his knees in front of her.

It was all Renae could do not to pull down the tight, elastic waist of the costume bottoms and let him continue what he was doing.

A light seemed to brighten his eyes. "Sting."

Renae frowned. The pop singer Sting was not exactly what she had in mind when it came to belly-dancing music. But Will was already in front of his stereo console, searching through an extensive collection of CDs then feeding one into the player.

Immediately the sound of Middle Eastern music filled the condo, along with the voice of an Arabic singer.

"Desert Rose by Sting," Will elaborated.

While it wasn't the exact belly-dancing beat she'd been looking for, she determined that she could make it work. Hell, at this point, with Will looking at her like he wanted to swallow her whole, she probably could have shaken her hips to Barbra Streisand, and Will and she would have been satisfied.

Shaking out her arms, she stretched them in front of her. Then she joined her index fingers and lifted her hands above her head. She found the stretch helped loosen up her muscles and get her into the mood. She slowly swung her left hip forward and began a tiny gyration, the disks sewn into the costume clinking.

She watched Will's eyes darken as she caught her rhythm. Slow at first. Concentrating on one hip, then the next. Rippling her stomach in a way that made it impossible for him to look anywhere but there. She shimmied her shoulders, threading her hands out in open invitation even as she gently threw her head back. She drew on the experience that teaching the classes had given her but which she seldom got to use in its intended way. Heat curled deep in her belly, making her hot. Too hot.

She leveled the tilt of her head, looking at him from under the fringe of her lashes as she increased the rhythm of her suggestive movements, making the disks clink faster.

"Fuck me."

Renae nearly burst out laughing. She knew the expletive was the British equivalent of "shit" or "what the hell," not meant to be taken literally. But she wasn't so sure if that's the meaning Will had intended as he practically dove at her. He pinned her to the overstuffed cushions of his sofa in a tangle of limbs and noisy disks.

"Wait," she whispered breathlessly after fighting to keep up with his kisses and batting his hands away from her costume. "Do you know how much this thing cost? Ginger would kill me if I ruined it."

"I'll buy you ten."

She laughed and bit his bottom lip.

"Ow. What did you go and do that for?"

"Give me a minute."

"Another one? But I just gave you one."

"You gave me twenty seconds."

He reluctantly pulled back. "Fine. I'll give you the other forty. But only if you promise not to take them all."

Renae got up and got out of the costume as quickly as she could. Before she could finish draping the top over a nearby chair, Will was tackling her back to the sofa. She caught herself on all fours just as he positioned himself behind her.

She thought about making a crack about his impatience for all of a nanosecond, but found she didn't have the time to voice anything as his hands curved around her waist then dove for her sex. She gasped as he parted her flesh with one hand, then skillfully stroked her bared feminine folds with the fingers of his other one.

"Oh, you're good," she whispered, every inch of her shivering in instant response to his attentions.

"You have no idea."

Renae leaned back, bearing against him. "Oh, I think I have an idea. But if it's all the same to you, I think I could do without repeating the beginning of the last time."

He chuckled against her back then thrust two fingers deep inside her slick opening. Renae gasped, the chaos swirling inside her gaining momentum. Her eyelids drifted closed and she felt a peculiar type of heat suffuse her muscles.

"Mmm...so tight...so wet."

Will twisted his fingers as he withdrew them then thrust them back up, stretching her muscles, readying her for him.

It was eight o'clock on a Monday morning and Renae was about to have sex with Will on his couch. The total sinfulness of the act set her nerve endings on fire and made her take a look at life through slightly askew glasses. She was normally so responsible, so focused. But one depraved grin from Will and she was calling in sick and stripping naked so he could have his way with her.

So she could have her way with him.

Reaching between her legs, she decided she'd had enough foreplay. She wanted to feel him inside her now. This instant.

She was slightly surprised to find him already sheathed as she grasped his hard girth and guided the knob of his arousal to her dripping entrance. He slid his fingers from her and replaced them with his erection, nearly driving her straight over the edge with the first thrust.

Oh, yes… This was definitely better than work. Better than being a responsible adult living a responsible life. The utter recklessness of her actions left her feeling powerful and different and…alive, for the first time in so very long that she wanted it to last and last.

Will seemed to tune in to her needs as he slowly withdrew, drawing out the action so that she was aware of every beat of her heart, every wash of blood through her veins, every molecule of oxygen she pulled into her lungs. He placed one hand at the small of her back and the other on her hip, holding her still when she might have bore back on him. Then he entered her again just as slowly, torturously, filling her to overflowing, making her feel as substantial as a puddle of melting hormones.

She heard a long, low moan and realized it was her own as sweet, unbearable pressure built up in her lower abdomen. A pressure that spiked with each of Will's skillful strokes. The feel of his white leather sofa was soft under her knees and palms, the heat of his flesh hot against her backside. She wanted—needed—him to increase the pace, her mind suspended between sensation and a desire for release so intense she lost track of time and place. Will moved so that his right foot was on the floor and he continued his slow strokes…in…out…in… out.

Renae's breath hitched high in her throat, making her think she might never take another normal breath again. Then the hand at the small of her back slid to her other hip and his grip increased enough for her to be aware of it. Just as she registered the change, he thrust into her to the hilt, his rhythm not only increasing, but his strokes growing more powerful, demanding. She arched her back and bore back against him. He held her still as he thrust deeply again and again, creating a kaleidoscope of color on the back of her eyelids, launching her into a parallel world that was pure sensation and fundamental human need. With each of his thrusts, her breasts swayed and the slap of his flesh against hers grew louder, challenging the volume of her low moans.

"Christ, what you do to me."

Will's words foretold his crisis and precipitated hers, the tension in her exploding, the chaos taking over her body and swirling and swirling around, her stomach convulsing, her lungs straining to take in a breath. But rather than stop his movements, Will increased the tempo of his strokes, his groan mingling with her moan.

And making Renae wish he would never stop.

THREE HOURS LATER Will lay with the back of his head hanging over the foot of his bed while Renae lay crosswise across the mattress, her legs entangled with his. He'd barely had had any sleep for a good twenty hours, and then he'd put in a grueling twelve-hour shift at the hospital during which he'd treated no fewer than seven teenagers apparently involved in some sort of gang dispute, and four car accident victims, one of whom had been life-flighted in. But damned if he felt tired. Sated, maybe. Horny, definitely. But not tired.

Even as he grinned like a fool, he thought there

was something wrong there. While sex had always been important to him, he'd never felt such an insatiable need to have it with one woman for long, uninterrupted hours without a break. But he'd be damned if even after three hours and countless orgasms he didn't want to roll Renae over and have at her again.

He lifted his head and zoned in on her pert, supple backside. The hell with turning her over. He'd take her like that.

The bedding rustled as she turned her head to look in his direction, her flushed, smiling face mirroring what he felt.

"Wow," she said.

Will had a hard time swallowing as he let his head loll back over the side of the bed. "Quite definitely wow."

He was aware that Renae was trying to free her right leg from where it was pinned under his, but she wasn't making much of an effort and he couldn't seem to scare up the energy to allow her the freedom. Instead she rolled over and he watched through half-lidded eyes as she pushed herself up into a sitting position.

"You know I'm not a lesbian, don't you?"

Will's brows rose. "Pardon me?"

She made two attempts before she was able to both balance herself and push her hair from her face. "Tabitha and I are just roommates. We're not a couple in the romantic sense. In fact, I guess you didn't realize it but Tabitha has a girlfriend named Nina, who lives with us, too."

Will made a face and shifted until his head was supported by the mattress. "Well, there goes my favorite fantasy."

She smiled in his general direction.

Will pulled in a deep breath then let it out slowly. "I sort of guessed as much. I mean, if you were a true lesbian, you wouldn't have slept with me, much less stuck around following our…unfortunate beginning."

The mattress began to shake although Will heard no sound. He realized she was laughing. "What's that supposed to mean?"

He shrugged and folded his arms under the back of his head. "Oh, I don't know. I suppose every now and again even homosexuals desire sex with those they normally wouldn't. But if you were truly gay, after my…Quick Withdraw McGraw routine, as you so rudely put it, well, a true homosexual probably would have shaken her head and left, her belief in the opposite sex's inability to perform confirmed."

Renae's laughing presumably took so much of her sapped energy she could no longer support her upright position. She fell solidly back to the bed, making Will's head bounce. When her laughter finally subsided, she repositioned herself until she was stretched out next to him. They weren't touching, but for some odd reason Will felt closer to the woman next to him than he'd felt to another person in a long, long time. He almost finished that thought with the words "if ever," but ignored them, not about to go there.

"Has anyone ever told you you're narrow-minded?" she asked, reaching for a pillow off the floor and bunching it under her head.

Will tried to steal the pillow. "I'm not narrow-minded. I'm subjective."

Renae swatted his hand away from her pillow. "Which means?"

Will finally gave up on the pillow and, using his feet and hands, grabbed his own from the other side of the bed. "Meaning I see things the way I want to see them. If I chose to see things the way you see them, then, well, my lesbian fantasy wouldn't hold any water now, would it? Because a true lesbian wouldn't be attracted to the opposite sex no matter how sexy." He waggled his brows at her. "Which brings me back to my sensing that you weren't truly a lesbian."

He watched as she twisted her lips. "You have a convoluted way of thinking. But at least it takes you where you need to be." She turned her head to look at him. "Tabitha *is* a lesbian, however."

Will found the energy to turn to his side and prop his head on his hand. "Do tell."

Her green eyes sparkled at him.

"Maybe my lesbian fantasy doesn't have to die a slow and torturous death after all."

She pulled the pillow from behind her head and whacked him with it. After she was settled again, she fell silent for a long moment, apparently mapping out the tiny lines in the ceiling.

Then she finally said, "So…tell me about the resident."

7
_____

ONE MINUTE WILL FELT like he was drifting on a warm ocean wave with nothing more important to do than stay afloat, the next a big white shark had come out of nowhere and made a beeline for his privates.

"Uh-oh. Wrong question?"

Will suddenly found it difficult to swallow. "No…no. Not so much a wrong question, really, as the wrong time."

Renae rolled to her side to face him. "Well, seeing as whenever we're together we're in bed, when would be the right time?"

Will couldn't bring himself to look directly into her eyes. "Oh, I don't know. Never?"

And just like that all the humor was drained out of the moment for him.

Oh, he didn't mistake himself for an angel by any stretch, but it had been a good long time since he'd viewed cheating on a girlfriend as acceptable behavior. Well, maybe not so much acceptable as understandable. There had been the time in med school when the hot anatomy teacher had offered to give him a tour of her own private anatomy and to demonstrate her considerable knowledge of the male anatomy, and Will had been loath to refuse the offer, despite that he was dating a fellow student at the time. And another occasion when a close friend of another girl he'd been dating had let spill her fantasies about him, and he'd found recreating them in reality momentarily irresistible.

But all that had transpired years ago when he'd been young and brash and a slave to his libido. Surely even he had grown up a little since.

He drew in a deep breath and slowly released it. Explain then how he'd been able to talk to Janet on the phone for a good half hour the night before, offering a sympathetic ear to her complaints about the hotel staff and the loss of her notes. Renae and their shenanigans had not even entered on the fringes of his mind, just as when he was with Renae, Janet didn't even rate a passing thought.

He grimaced at the thought.

The bedding rustled and he looked at where Renae was lying on her stomach, her chin buried in the middle of her pillow while she considered the wall-to-wall carpeting. Will couldn't resist a visual sweep of her gloriously bare body, from her tanned feet to her rounded rump to her smooth shoulders and dark blond hair.

"You and the resident have a good sex life?" she asked.

Now there was a question. "Actually we don't have a sex life. At least not one to speak of...yet." Curious how the "yet" almost didn't seem connected to the rest of his sentence. It was more of an afterthought than a given.

He watched her brows raise then she turned her head on the pillow and smiled at him. "None?"

He shook his head.

Her smile widened and he had the feeling he was going to regret letting that particular cat out of the bag. "Well, then, there's really no need for the guilt written across your face now, is there?"

Will blinked at her, as if bringing her into sharper focus would have the same effect on her words. "Pardon me?"

She shifted until she lay on her side again, wonderfully unconcerned with her nakedness. "There's a point in there somewhere. Would you like me to explain it to you?"

There were a lot of other things he wanted her to do but he supposed he really should start with that. "Mmm. Yes, I would."

"Well, you're feeling bad because you're in bed with me while we discuss the resident."

"Go on."

"My point is that if you're not sleeping with her, then you're not being unfaithful to her."

"Interesting point." That did absolutely nothing to erase his feeling of guilt.

"No, really. Think about it. Until the both of you commit physically, well, then it's impossible for you to be physically unfaithful."

"So following your reasoning, a man about to go to the altar is free to do what he wants until he utters the words 'I do.'"

She laughed. "No, silly. An agreement is implied then. An engagement." Her eyes widened. "There's no ring involved with you and the resident, is there?"

"No."

"Whew. Thank God. You scared me for a minute there."

"Yes, well, consider what you're doing to me."

She pushed up onto her elbow and looked at him. "This is really bothering you, isn't it?"

"No," he lied. "The fact that I'm discussing it with you is a cause of some concern, though."

Her eyes danced with light. "Because I'm the other woman."

"Because you're lying naked in my bed."

"Ah."

"Yes, very definitely 'ah.'"

She twisted her lips, emphasizing how very full

and kissable they were. "Would you like me to leave?"

Surprisingly their conversation had momentarily impacted Big Ben's control over Will. But as he looked at the pert tips of Renae's breasts, the smooth skin of her stomach, the neat triangle of hair between her legs, Ben was quickly reasserting his dominance.

"No."

"So you want me to stay then?"

"No," he said just as quickly.

She laughed. "Well, since I'm not about to hide in your closet if, when and until you decide, maybe I'd better go."

"No," he said again, gripping her arm when she might have rolled off the other side of the bed.

He gazed into her face, thinking of how incredibly sexy she was. How inappropriately irresistible. While he may have been unfaithful to women before, even the anatomy teacher and the friend of his ex hadn't managed to keep his attention for longer than a couple of hours.

But Renae…

It was going on the fourth hour of his second sexual tryst with her and not only wasn't he tiring of Renae Truesdale's company, he wanted more of it. Of her.

"I've got an interesting question for you," he said quietly.

"Oh?"

"Don't you think it a bit odd that you're not jealous of…the resident?" He winced at following Renae's lead and calling Janet "the resident" rather than referring to her by name. But Janet wasn't the topic of conversation right now. Rather Renae and her curious behavior were what interested him.

"Jealous?"

"Mmm. I mean, for all intents and purposes I'm dating someone else. And while I might not have had sex with her…yet," he forced himself to add, "I've wanted to."

"And because of that I should be jealous?"

"Well…yes. Wouldn't that be the normal human reaction to the situation?"

"Depends on your definition of normal."

He conceded the point. "So yours differs from most everyone else's then?"

"Maybe it isn't the definition so much as the circumstances. And the circumstances in this particular situation—"

"Our situation."

"—are that I knew you were involved with someone when we began having sex."

"Mmm. But that doesn't explain why you're not

jealous now that we've surpassed one-night stand territory.''

Her laughter, which usually inspired in him lustful thoughts, now seemed to rub him the wrong way. ''I wouldn't classify what's going on as a long-term relationship, Will.''

''No, I don't suppose you would.''

She remained silent for long moments, the smile slipping from her face as she openly considered him. ''Would you? Classify this as a relationship?''

''Well, there lies the dilemma, doesn't it?''

''I'm not following you.''

He sighed heavily and ran his hand over his face. He needed a shave, a shower. But he couldn't seem to scare up the energy for either.

He looked at where Renae's belly ring glinted up at him, calling his attention to her supple abdomen, her smooth flesh. He idly wondered how he even had the energy to think about taking up where they'd left off.

''Of course you're not following me,'' he offered up. ''Simply because I don't know where in the hell I'm going with this, either.''

The uncomfortable feeling in the pit of his gut had him worried. He supposed it was only natural considering the situation he'd put himself in. It was guilt, plain and simple.

He glanced at the woman next to him. Then again, it could be something else entirely.

"Are you seeing anybody?" he asked.

RENAE FELT LAUGHTER bubble up from her chest.

Will and his obvious struggle with morality was nothing if not the cutest thing she'd ever witnessed.

"Excuse me?" she asked.

He waved his hand. "I mean, I know we've already established that you're not involved with your roommate. But is there…a man anywhere in the picture?"

"Hmm. A man."

He really was having trouble with this, wasn't he?

Renae propped her head on her hand. When she'd agreed to play hooky from work—something she'd never even thought about doing before, much less did—to spend the day in bed with Will, the last thing she would have expected was this peculiar conversation.

"If you're asking if I'm dating anyone, my answer would have to be no."

"Engaged in a harmless flirtation?"

She laughed. "No."

"Talking to an old flame on the phone?"

"No."

"Fixed some poor sap in your sights?"

"No."

He looked strangely relieved and disappointed by the news simultaneously.

"I'm currently man-free." She reached out and smoothed his hair back from his forehead. "Present company excepted, of course."

"Mmm. Of course." He turned his head to look at her. "And you're truly not jealous. Not in the least."

Renae's hand hesitated at his temple. Then she smiled, drew her finger along the line of his cheek then down to his jawline and kissed him. "Not in the least."

Now had he been sleeping with the resident…

Renae caught her mind traveling down the unwanted avenue and tried to draw it to a halt.

But the truth was that the instant he admitted that he and the woman he was dating weren't engaging in any sack sessions, that the resident hadn't spent the night in the bed they were currently in while she had spent a nice-size chunk of the past three days there…well, gave her a bit of satisfaction, however wicked.

Not that she'd ever let Will know that. Oh, no. No matter how deliciously tortured he looked, she wouldn't feed that tidbit to his enormous ego.

Speaking of enormous…her gaze dropped to his semierect male member that was large even in slumber. And a part of her was glad that she knew that over the resident. Liked that when she reached out, she could touch the warm flesh, watching as it grew thicker, more erect. Reveled in the feel of its hardness in her palm, a hardness caused by her and her actions.

"So tell me more about these fantasies you used to have about me and Tabitha," she coaxed, her mouth watering with the desire to taste him against her tongue.

Will groaned as she completely encircled his girth and gave a calculated squeeze. "'Used to have' being the key words," he said, dipping his chin into his chest so he could watch her. "But of course you shot all that down by revealing you weren't a lesbian. Or at least bi. Bi would have been nice. Because it means you—"

Renae scooted closer to him and pressed her tongue against the head of his need. She looked up at him. "Has anyone ever told you you talk too much?"

"No. Never. Perhaps it's nerves. Or guilt. Guilt does the strangest things to—"

Renae moved her mouth over the head of his arousal and swirled her tongue along the sensitive rim, satisfied when his sentence ended in a low, needy groan.

She slid her mouth farther down his length and

applied suction, then released him. "You were saying?"

"I was saying?" His eyes had a faraway look in them. "To hell with what I was saying. Just continue."

She gave a quiet chuckle and did just that.

8

THE FOLLOWING NIGHT Will was no closer to making sense out of what was going on inside his head than he'd been the morning before—with or without Renae's decadent mouth on his person.

He swept through the waiting area of St. Vincent Mercy Medical Center, not willing any ill fortune on the general population but wishing things were a little busier so he could occupy his mind with something other than the dilemma he was currently facing. He'd been on the job for an hour and it felt like he'd been there at least ten.

He ran into first-year resident Evan Hadley coming out of one of the examining rooms. "Hey," Will said. "Anything interesting happening?"

Evan had everything going for him: good-looking, clever, with the type of all-American football-hero grin that made the nurses swoon. Will would have hated him on sight if he hadn't been instrumental in bringing the resident on board as a favor to one of his college professors.

Besides, the nurses had swooned over Will in the

beginning, too. But once someone on the staff reached the one-year point, and fresh blood came in, the previous object of the nurses' affection was cast aside.

Evan was shaking his head. "Nope. Nosebleed."

Will made a face. "That's about as exciting as it gets tonight."

Evan nodded as he made a notation on the chart he held. "Makes me wish I was still in L.A. Even a boring medical convention is more interesting than this."

Will pointed at him. "That's right. You attended the first weekend, didn't you? Did you run into Janet?"

"Once or twice in the hall." He shrugged. "What's it look like today from your side of the center?"

"Even more dead than on your side."

Evan began walking toward the nurses' station. "I guess we should hope it stays that way."

"I guess."

Will glanced at his watch, conversed with a couple of the nurses about ongoing cases, then walked back toward the locker room, his thoughts circling back to Renae. He tried to convince himself that it was the void that allowed her entrance, but the truth was he couldn't seem to shake her from his mind no matter how hard he tried.

Despite his strange conversation with her the day before, precipitated by her asking about Janet, they'd gone on to spend not only the remainder of that morning in bed having phenomenal sex, but the rest of the day, getting up only to raid the fridge and place a call for Chinese delivery. And they'd ordered lots of it, because not only did everyone know that you were hungry again a half hour after eating Chinese food, but at the rate he and Renae were burning calories, they'd needed the sustenance.

Funny, he'd never factored in pure exhaustion as a reason to stop having sex.

At somewhere around four in the afternoon he'd fallen into a dead sleep only to wake to the sound of the alarm at seven-thirty…alone. No note. No panties left behind on his bedside lamp. No sign that Renae had been there at all.

Well, except for his memories, his tired muscles and her scent, which seemed to be everywhere.

The maddening woman was out to drive him insane. He could feel it in his bones.

And the idea that she was in it only for the sex bothered him on some level he was reluctant to pursue.

"Bugger."

That didn't make any sense, now, did it, it bothering him that she was after him just for the sex?

After all, he was only in it for the sex, so why shouldn't Renae feel the same way? His judging her actions as somehow…questionable emerged as downright sexist. The whole what's good for the goose is not good for the gander argument. The man was a stud, the woman a slut syndrome.

He slapped the chart he was carrying down on the round table then sat in one of the five chairs, the locker room blessedly empty at the beginning of the shift. In an hour or so the opposite would be true as the night staff began coming and going, restlessness settling in.

Only Will's restlessness seemed to be a constant presence these days.

He didn't find it the least bit amusing that it had been his restlessness, his sexual frustration, that had chased him into Renae's arms to begin with. Now it was Renae's arms—and his not wanting to leave them—that were the cause of his restlessness.

Colin had been right to stay out of this one. Hell, if *he* could find a way out, he'd take it.

If only Renae had been the least bit clingy… asked him to stop seeing Janet…displayed just a hint of jealousy, he suspected everything would be different.

And there lay the quandary.

Will had never believed himself to be shallow. But he couldn't help thinking if he was—if men in general were—it was because of the women they dated. He'd faced his share of scornful women who had willingly shared his bed one night, knowing there would be nothing beyond that and then had hated him when he didn't call them the next day anyway.

Was the reason why he'd sought Renae out after the first time because she hadn't expected him to call? Hadn't expected anything from him, period?

Will rested his head against his hand and scratched his temple. If that was the case then there was more than a little merit to those books on dating rules and the whole Mars-Venus angle that he'd scoffed at such a short time ago. Could it be true that all women had to do was play hard to get? Make the man feel like he had to work to get her attention, and—bam!—the man in question was a goner?

Another curious question began forming in the back of his mind. Would he even still be dating Janet had she slept with him early on in their relationship?

He glanced at his watch again. Oh, boy, this was certainly getting him nowhere fast.

Of course, the mind-set of the woman in question would actually have to be for real. Janet genuinely wanted to wait for her wedding night. Renae was genuinely in it just for the sex. He didn't think he'd be struggling with thoughts of either of them—or thinking about them at all—had he sensed that they were playing games. Like if Renae showed even a hint of "I'm pretending I don't care, but I'm just playing with you, but could you call tomorrow anyway?" Or if he saw in Janet anything that equaled, "I'm not giving you sex because it's my way of manipulating you into paying for the most expensive wedding this side of the Atlantic."

Then there was another question: Was it possible to want two different women for two completely different reasons?

He glanced toward the sealed window at the dark night beyond. Was it possible for him to be in any worse shape?

There was a brief knock on the door and then it opened inward, revealing Janet's father, Dr. Stuart Nealon, who also just happened to be the head of staff at the hospital.

Will swallowed hard as he scrambled to a standing position.

"Will, there you are," Stuart said, his face looking stern. "I was hoping we could have a talk, you and I. Man to man."

Oh, yeah, he realized with growing dread, it was very possible for things to get worse. And they just had.

RENAE FOLDED thick Turkish terry cloth robes and stacked them on the display shelf at Women Only, her thoughts as far away as where the robes had come from. Before she knew it, she reached the bottom of the shipping box and stood for long moments blinking as if unsure what to do with it.

"The robes are nice, but they're not that nice."

She looked up to find Lucky coming into the main showroom from the dance room. Lately the pretty redhead had been coming in after-hours to do some stretching and simple calisthenics, claiming she needed to wind down after a long day of trying to get her shop together downtown…and before she went home to Colin.

Renae smiled and shook her head. "Sorry, what did you say? I just can't seem to concentrate on anything lately."

Lucky came to lean against the checkout counter, her gaze homing in on Renae's face. "I was just commenting on your distractedness." She took the box from her and began collapsing it so it would fit in the Dumpster out back.

"I was hoping Ginger would come by tonight. She's barely been in the shop all week and…" And Renae had been hoping to talk to her.

Lucky squinted at her. "Look, Renae, there's obviously something going on that I don't know about, something you've been reluctant to talk about.''

Was it that obvious? Renae picked up some packing material from the floor.

"I just wanted to let you know that if you need an ear, I'm here, you know?''

She stood up and took in the genuine affection on Lucky's face. "I know,'' she said quietly.

And that's exactly when she decided to talk.

But it wasn't about Will and their…strange but exciting rendezvous, even though he seemed to be taking up more and more of her thought space recently. Rather for the first time since the idea had taken root, she poured out to Lucky all her professional hopes, all her dreams.

"I don't know where to start,'' she said, deciding the beginning would be best. "When Ginger took me on five years ago, I never thought beyond the next minute. You know, stock the shelves, come up with new ideas that women might be interested in—''

"Give massages, teach belly-dancing classes,'' Lucky added with a warm smile.

"Exactly. Everything was going fine. I mean, I was happy with my job. Happy working with Ginger.''

"But…''

Renae hadn't realized she'd fallen silent until

Lucky prompted her. "But…no, not but. I'm still very happy here. I can't think of any place else I'd like to work. It's just that…my interest has evolved."

"Interest in the shop?"

Renae nodded, stared at where she still held the packing material in her hands then rounded the counter to throw it away. "First Leah Westwood announces plans to open a sister shop near Sylvania. I mean, I knew she was part owner here, but…"

"Then you hired me on…." Lucky lead on.

Renae smiled at her. "You know where I'm going with this, don't you?"

"Mmm. I suspect I've known since before even you realized it." She drew up beside her and slung an arm around her. "You don't want to merely work here anymore, you want to buy into Women Only. Or maybe even open a sister shop of your own."

Renae stared at her.

Lucky smiled. "What's say we go into the parlor and talk about this over a cup of ginseng tea?"

Despite the added weight to her shoulders caused by Lucky's arm, Renae felt like a hundred pounds had been lifted from her. Now that she'd spoken the words aloud, her hopes and her dreams didn't seem like some sort of wispy, insubstantial fog, but a solid ladder leading to heights unknown.

And as Renae followed Lucky into the other room, she discovered her heart was pounding with the desire to climb as high as she could go.

"WHERE DO THINGS STAND between you and my daughter?"

Will blinked at the elder Nealon. Upon hunting Will down, er, finding him in the staff locker room, he'd suggested they go to the cafeteria for coffee and a doughnut. Will had skipped the doughnut, and wished he'd gone for the decaffeinated coffee because his nerves were already stretched taut, his hand nearly shaking when he lifted the paper cup to his lips.

"Pardon me?" he very nearly croaked.

Stuart grinned. "Did you think you'd be able to keep your dating Janet from me for long?"

Will put his cup down and shook his head, trying for a casual grin of his own. "No, sir, I didn't. I just didn't think you'd find out about us so soon."

In all honesty, he hadn't been thinking at all when it came to Janet's connection to the hospital chief of staff. It had been two weeks into their dating that he'd even learned of the connection. And by then he'd already been knee-deep into his plan to seduce the pretty resident.

"Yes, well, I've actually known for some time.

Since the beginning, in fact. You see, my daughter and I don't have many secrets.''

Will was glad he hadn't been sipping coffee just then or else he might have spewed it all over the other man.

''She made me promise not to say anything to you, though.''

Then why was he telling him now?

Will absently rubbed his chin. ''Yes, well…I've grown very…fond of your daughter, sir.''

Stuart waved his hand. ''Enough with the 'sir' bit, Sexton. You've worked here for how long now?''

''Nearly six years, sir.'' And two years ago Stuart Nealon had been elevated to chief of staff.

Stuart's grin widened. ''I think that's long enough for us to advance to something more personal. Please call me Stuart.''

Will nodded. ''Stuart. Yes, right then. Stuart.''

Why was he getting the impression that Stuart was going to ask him what his intentions were toward his daughter? And just what ''secrets'' hadn't the two kept from each other? Did his boss know that he had yet to have sex with his daughter? Or did he think the two of them were going at it at every opportunity?

Stuart's stern face didn't give anything away. Will knew that one didn't rise to Stuart's level without having learned a certain amount of self-control—and a really good poker face.

"Anyway, as luck would have it Janet is not the reason I wanted to speak to you."

Will fought not to blink. "Oh?"

"Yes. You see, I've had my eye on you for some time now, Sexton." He shook his finger at him. "You've made quite an impression on me and on everyone you work with."

Will's ego inflated at the bit of flattery even as a warning alarm went off in the back of his head.

"I seem to recall your being interested in a day position in the trauma center...."

"Um, yes, sir. I mean, Stuart. I was and am still very much interested."

Stuart smiled. "Good. Keep your nose clean, boy, and you just might get what you want."

The older physician stood up and Will followed suit even though he was afraid his knees were knocking together so hard the other man would hear them.

That was it? That's what Stuart had wanted to speak to him about? To tell him he was being considered for the day slot?

Or was his mission to hint, keep his daughter happy and Will would in turn be given a chance at professional happiness?

Oh, what a tangled web we weave, Will thought.

"Pardon?" Stuart asked as he led the way out.

Will blinked at him. "Sir? I didn't say anything."

At least he hoped like hell he hadn't said anything. Because everything he'd been working toward for the past six years hung in the balance.

9

THE FOLLOWING DAY was Renae's usual day off and she'd decided to use it to take Lucky up on her advice and come up with a written plan for Ginger to consider. A plan that would give her the option, over time, of buying interest in the shop. A plan that would take her into the future.

The future...

Now that was a concept she hadn't given much consideration to before. Even now—as she lay across Will's bed, spent and sated, one of his legs crossing hers—tomorrow loomed large and mysterious and more than a bit exciting.

"I always wondered what that song 'Afternoon Delight' meant."

Renae chuckled quietly at Will's joke, rolling her ankle to knock it against his. "We've had sex in the afternoon."

"Yes, but until now it usually started at another point. You know, in the morning...the night before..."

Renae's smile felt plastered to her face.

The last person she'd expected to see at her door an hour earlier had been Will. She'd thought that since he'd worked last night, he'd be asleep. Instead he'd stood at the door looking as irresistible as a double-double chocolate brownie and invited her down to his place for a quickie—he'd said it with an irresistible waggle of his brows that indicated there would be nothing quick about it. Since she'd already put together a lot of what she hoped to present to Ginger, she'd decided she needed the break. The emphasis on break. She intended to be back in her condo by five o'clock in order to put the finishing touches on her proposal.

She felt a hot, meandering hand on her inner thigh and moved her head to watch as Will inched his way toward her throbbing sex.

"I can't believe you. Aren't you tired? You already admitted you haven't gotten any sleep since knocking off work this morning." She glanced at the slender watch still on her wrist, the only thing that remained from what she'd had on an hour earlier. "Seeing as you have to be back at work in four hours…"

"Are you saying you'd rather sleep?"

His fingers reached her swollen womanhood, the tips following the folds of closed flesh then coaxing them open. A shiver worked its way up from Renae's toes, hitting every spot in between. "I'm saying that maybe you should think about getting some sleep.'' She swallowed hard as he drew his fingers through her slick channel. ''I mean, if I foul up on the job, someone gets a wrong size robe. You screw up, a scalpel shows up on X-ray the next day.''

He lightly pinched her hooded flesh. ''Very funny.''

Renae giggled and moved out of reach, suddenly feeling the desire to talk to him. Just talk. She propped her head on her hand and handed him a pillow, which he took and put under his head. ''Did something happen that you want to talk about?''

His brows rose high on his forehead, drawing her attention to his sexily disheveled hair, his naughty eyes. ''What makes you ask something like that?''

She shrugged. ''I don't know. You seem…a little distracted today, that's all.''

He lifted up onto his elbows. ''Are you implying that I've been derelict in my sexual duties?''

''No. That's not what I mean at all.''

He made a sound of satisfaction. ''That's what I thought.''

Renae lay back and stared at the ceiling. ''Conceited. Definitely conceited.''

''Confident. There's a difference, you know.''

He reached for her again and she laughed and moved out of touching distance. ''You can't possibly want to have sex again.''

"Why can't I?"

"Well, for one, I think we finished plowing through every last chapter in the *Kama Sutra* sometime yesterday."

"And your point is?"

"My point is…"

What was her point?

For a moment there, Renae had mistaken Will as someone who was interested in more than sex from her.

And for a moment there, she'd made the mistake of thinking she was interested in more than sex from him.

He rolled to his side. "Uh-oh. What's going on in that pretty little head of yours?"

Renae opened her mouth then snapped it back closed. She realized with a start that she was a breath away from sharing her plans for Women Only with him. Telling him how frustrating it was that she hadn't yet been able to catch up with Ginger. About how Lucky had made her see the light yesterday and she was planning on calling Ginger later that day to make an actual lunch date so she could pitch her proposal to her flat out. Tell him that spread out upstairs on the kitchen table were her scribbled ideas and plans and all she had to do was put them into some comprehensible order.

"Actually you're right," she said. "I don't have a point."

She began getting up and he curved his fingers around her bare ankle and tugged. "Where are you going?"

"Back to my place. You need some sleep."

"Oh, no, you don't."

He pulled her until she lay alongside him then he pinned her to the bed, hovering above her like some sort of sexy British god. She tried to keep her smile from showing but failed.

"Get off of me right now. You're smooshing me."

He waggled his brows. "You've never complained about my smooshing you before."

"That's because I wanted you to smoosh me then."

"And you don't now?"

Renae caught her bottom lip between her teeth and bit down, his skin against hers making her remember how very much she loved having sex with him. "No."

His expression went suddenly serious. "No?"

He began releasing her.

Renae took the opportunity to trade positions with him and pin him to the bed.

"All that so you could be on top?" he asked as she straddled his hips, putting her sex in direct contact with his. "Completely unnecessary. All you had to do was ask."

Renae leaned in to kiss him.

"Now that's more like it," he said.

The telephone on the bedside table chirped.

They ignored it.

Renae reached toward the opposite bedside table and fished a fresh condom out of the drawer. She ripped it open then held it up above Will's eyes like bait. "Are you sure this is what you want?"

"Give me that rubber."

The telephone continued to ring even as Will grabbed the condom from her fingers.

"Persistent," Renae said, gasping when he sucked on one of her nipples.

"Rejection. They'll get used to it."

The telephone finally stopped its incessant ringing and Renae relaxed, scooting back so Will could put on the condom.

"Now, where were we?"

The telephone instantly began ringing again.

"Bugger," Will cursed.

Renae rolled off him and he took that to mean he should get it.

"Maybe they need you at the hospital," she suggested.

"I have a beeper for that."

"Oh."

Very definitely "oh," Will thought as he sat on the side of the bed and snatched up the receiver.

"This had bloody well better be good," he said into the receiver.

"Will? I'm sorry, did I wake you?"

He shot from the bed so fast you would have thought he'd been catapulted.

Janet.

Jesus Christ and all his Apostles.

"I figured you'd probably be up by now and I had a break between seminars and thought I'd call, you know, to see how you're doing."

He listened to Janet apologize for waking him when he'd been nowhere near asleep but rather about to continue banging the hell out of his upstairs neighbor. Will stared at where Renae lay across his bed like a siren waiting for him to respond to her tempting song.

He quickly turned from Renae and the bed and paced toward the nearby bathroom.

Shit, shit, shit.

He heard the cradle of the telephone hit the floor, having inadvertently pulled it from the night table.

"Will? What was that?"

He picked up the cradle, tugged on the line to make sure he had enough give, then headed into the bathroom. "I dropped the phone."

"Hard night?"

Will closed his eyes tightly, remembering that Renae had pretty much asked him the same question a few minutes ago. ''No…no, it was fine. I was just a little late getting to sleep after I knocked off this morning, that's all.''

''Because you missed me?''

Will met Renae's curious gaze from the bed as if she'd heard the question Janet had asked.

He closed the bathroom door and leaned against it. ''Yeah…that must be it.''

''Aw, that's sweet. I miss you, too.''

How much? was on the tip of his tongue. Where, thankfully, the words stayed.

''Are you still coming to pick me up from the airport this Sunday?'' Janet asked.

Sunday. It loomed so far away yet somehow seemed too soon. ''Sure, yes.''

There was a long pause as Will tried to listen through the wood for what Renae might be doing in the other room.

''Will? Is everything all right?'' Janet asked.

He was everything but. ''Fine, fine,'' he said instead. ''I just need to hit the toilet and catch a shower is all.''

''Okay. I won't keep you then. My seminar starts in a couple of minutes anyway and I want to get a good seat up front.''

Good ole Janet, half a country away in California

with nothing more serious on her mind than getting a front row seat.

He really was a cad.

"Okay. Have a good seminar, then."

"I will, thanks. Goodbye."

"Bye."

Will began to put the receiver into the cradle of the phone he held in his other hand, then lifted it back to his ear only to change his mind again and finally hang it up.

Well, wasn't that just peachy?

He usually remembered to forward all his calls to voice mail when Renae was over, and if he'd needed a reminder of why, this was it. He'd been hoping to avoid this very incident.

But today he'd forgotten and he'd been caught smack-dab with his pants around his ankles.

He stared at his ankles. Worse, he wasn't even wearing pants. And pretty much hadn't been for the past five days.

He heard a soft knock on the other side of the bathroom door. He stepped away and opened it. There Renae stood wearing the same clothes she'd had on when he'd gone up to her place to tempt her down here an hour ago. The pink and white striped capris and white tank shouldn't have looked as sexy as they did but, well, there you had it.

"Was it something I said?" he asked, clutching the phone in front of him.

Renae smiled. "I've got to get back to my place."

"Yeah, right. I see."

But did he?

No, he realized, he didn't.

A man who had a firm grip on reality didn't date one woman and not have sex with her, and not date another while having the most incredible sex he'd ever had.

"Would you like me to see you out?"

Renae shook her head as she put on her other sandal, drawing his attention to her incredibly sexy, tanned foot with the neon-pink toenail polish. "Nope. I know the way."

"About tomorrow morning…"

She leaned in and kissed him, then worked her index finger between their lips in order to hold his closed presumably to keep him from finishing his sentence. "Tomorrow morning is tomorrow morning. Let's wait and see what happens then."

"Right. Okay."

He seemed to be saying those inane words a lot lately. But for the life of him, he couldn't seem to rattle another response out of his shell-shocked brain.

And somehow he got the impression that it

wasn't going to get any better from there. He'd made—or unmade—his damn bed, and he was just going to have to find a way to either lie in it or get rid of it altogether.

10

RENAE LET HERSELF BACK into her condo, puzzled that even though she'd had a great orgasm a few minutes ago, her body was restless, her mind preoccupied with Will and what had just happened.

For a moment there, she had been jealous.

A moment? The instant Will had leapt from the bed, pulled the phone off the nightstand, then disappeared in all his butt-naked glory into the bathroom so he might speak to the resident without Renae overhearing, she'd known an envy so strong it had taken her breath away.

Not good. Not good at all.

Renae closed the door after herself and put her keys on the hall table, looking for a measure of comfort from the familiarity of the condo she'd lived in with Tabitha for the past six months, but oddly not finding it. Part of the reason might have been Nina's having redecorated the entire place. The soothing earth tones had been ''spiced up,'' as Nina put it, with garish neon-orange pillows and lime-colored throws, making Renae blanch whenever she took a look around the place. But since Tabitha didn't seem to mind the changes, and when all was said and done the condo was hers, Renae had kept her tongue firmly in her mouth.

"Tabby?"

While there was no reason to expect her friend to be home from work yet, she always called out to let whomever was in the apartment know she was there. Since Nina had been laid off a month back, she was the one usually home, but somehow Renae had never warmed to the idea of calling out her name. There was no reason to pretend she liked the other woman. *She* wasn't sleeping with her.

Then again, her own judgment when it came to bed partners might also be a little off-center.

She headed for the kitchen. At least her proposal for Women Only would get her mind off everything. Will, Nina, Tabitha, the fact that if things continued on the way they were she would have to look for a place of her own whether or not Tabby needed financial help. The simple fact was, she felt like a stranger in her own apartment. And that wasn't a good place to be no matter how you viewed it.

Since the afternoon sun had arced to the other side of the building, she had to switch on the overhead light in the kitchen. And the instant she did, she became aware of something amiss.

The kitchen table was empty, nothing but a fresh bowl of fruit where her notes had been.

Renae's heart did a little flip in her chest.

She rushed to the table, looked around the chairs, then opened the drawer from which she'd gotten the pad and pen. The pad and pen were there, neatly tucked away, as if she'd never used them, the pad not even showing the indents from her words on the top page.

"Nina?" she called out.

As she pulled out the garbage can that held that morning's empty orange juice container and butter wrapper she listened to the silence that greeted her in the condo.

She closed the cabinet door. This wasn't happening.

She turned and took in the room, then systematically made her way through the apartment, beginning with her bedroom where she hoped against hope that Nina had placed her notes on her dresser or bed, somewhere where she might find them. Nothing. She moved on through the dining and living rooms with the same result.

Outside the closed door to Tabitha and Nina's room, she paused. She'd never invaded Tabitha's privacy. If at night the door was open, and Tabitha invited her in, she went without hesitation, often stretching out on the bed next to her friend to catch an episode of *Northern Exposure* or *American Idol*. Of course, that had been before Nina moved in. After that…

Well, after that, Renae barely dared even to look through the open doorway for fear of what she might find. A rational fear since Nina seemed to get a great deal of joy out of moving about the place sans clothes, sometimes with no apparent reason at all. Being comfortable with one's body was one thing. Being an exhibitionist was quite another. And Nina fell solidly in the latter category.

And unfortunately she'd just added thief to the growing list of other names Renae had for her.

Bypassing Tabitha's bedroom, she stepped back into the kitchen and stood there staring at nothing and everything. She gathered the pad and pen from the cabinet drawer, backtracked to her own bedroom, then closed the door, vowing to be more careful about where she placed her things from here on out.

TWO DAYS LATER Renae sat across from Lucky at Coney Island Hot Dog on North Superior—the oldest restaurant in downtown Toledo if you were to believe the words on the window—picking at the contents of her plate, her mind a million miles away. She hadn't seen Will since the phone call incident at his place. Which probably had a lot to do with her going out of her way to avoid him. And his going out of his way to avoid her. Just this morning she'd been at the top of the third-floor stairs and stopped when she'd heard him enter. She'd listened to him check his mailbox—though there would be no mail that early—then climb the steps to his condo. But he must have lingered there in the hall after unlocking his door because she hadn't heard it close. Out of curiosity, she'd back-tracked to her condo door, opened it, then shut it. A split second later she'd heard his door close, and he'd been nowhere to be seen when she'd descended the stairs. Obviously he'd wanted no chance meeting.

What had she been thinking, getting involved with someone who lived in the same building?

Correction. She and Will were not involved. They'd had sex. And so long as she could continue to avoid him, and him her, well, there was no worry about any awkward moments.

She caught herself scratching her arm where it was left bare by her black tank top then caught sight of a spot of chili sauce on her white pants. She grimaced. Great, just great.

"You're awfully quiet today," Lucky said, her appetite apparently healthy as ever as she bit into her hot dog with gusto.

Renae had made an inventory delivery to Lucky's

blossoming shop a short ways away an hour ago and after spending some time going over other needs, Lucky had suggested they lunch at the popular hot dog place that, interestingly enough, sat smack-dab next to the swankiest restaurant Toledo had to offer.

"He's Georgio's and I'm Coney Island."

Lucky blinked at her and said around a full mouth, "What?"

Renae hadn't realized she'd said the words aloud until that moment. She waved her hand, picked up one of her own hot dogs, then chose a side and took a bite. "Will and I," she said, the food muffling her words. "He's Georgio's and I'm this hot dog place."

Lucky choked on a laugh and reached for her glass of soda. "You are not a hot dog place."

"Yes, I am. I'm a high school dropout who never even thought about getting her GED much less considered going on to college."

"And that makes you a hot dog place?"

She nodded and pointed her thumb in the direction of the wall that separated the two restaurants. "And Will's the gourmet place next door."

"How do you figure?"

Renae gave an eye roll and leaned forward. "Come on, Lucky, surely I don't have to spell it out to you."

"Indulge me."

"Fine. Will is a fancy restaurant because not only has he finished high school and college and med school, he's a friggin' doctor—a surgeon—for cripe's sake."

Lucky continued eating her hot dog as if they were discussing nothing more important than the weather, which currently happened to be hazy and hot, the restaurant's air-conditioning a draw for those looking to escape the August heat.

"I'm still not following the allegory."

"An analogy, I think." She put down her hot dog and crossed her forearms on top of the table. "You see, there's no skill needed in preparing a hot dog. What's there to do? You boil or broil the dogs, slap them in a bun, offer up a lot of condiments, throw in a bag of chips, and voila, an inexpensive meal is born. While Will…"

She'd done a lot of thinking about him, her and what had happened between them the past couple of days. Not because she'd wanted to. But rather she'd needed to. The other day she'd compared them to a bicycle and a BMW roadster. This morning she'd stared at the contents of the refrigerator and used tuna and salmon to demonstrate how they were different.

Now it was hot dogs and filet mignon.

"Will…well, he's a gourmet dish made up of

expensive ingredients, some of which it takes sniffing pigs in France to find, and each item has been carefully cut and prepared just so, taking time and patience and knowledge.''

''Mmm. As well as his being delicious,'' Lucky added.

''What's the matter with hot dogs?'' To prove her point, she picked up the one she was working on and filled her mouth with a bite.

Lucky smiled at her then cleared her throat when she realized Renae wasn't amused. ''Actually that was going to be my question. What is wrong with a hot dog? Providing, of course, that I'm accepting your comparing yourself to one?''

It took Renae a good minute to chew what was in her mouth then swallow before she could speak. ''Man cannot live on hot dogs alone?''

Lucky waggled her finger at her. ''Yes, but filet mignon isn't an American classic.''

''Will isn't American.''

This time Lucky burst out laughing, further deepening Renae's grimace.

''This is not funny.''

''I beg to differ. I find this entire conversation very amusing.'' She polished off her first hot dog then started on her second. ''If I were to buy what you're saying right now, Renae, well, then, I'd have to go home and boot Colin out of my apartment.''

"You two are living together?"

Lucky made a face. "Well, we haven't spent a night apart since working everything out two months ago, although neither of us has changed our mailing address." She waved her hand. "Anyway, back to my point. If it's your contention that hot dogs and filet mignon don't mix...well, then I've got a problem on my hands."

"You are so not a hot dog."

"And you are?"

Renae felt the beginnings of a smile take shape. "A really good hot dog. A popular one. What's that brand? The kind that plumps when you cook 'em? Or, no, wait. Maybe I'm a brat. Yeah, I like that better, I think."

"Will would say you were a banger."

"No, Will would say he wanted to bang me, but that's neither here nor there."

Renae felt better after a few minutes with her friend than she'd felt over the past few days. Not so much because of what they were saying, but rather because she was talking to someone at all. She'd been so busy with the shop, helping Lucky get ready for her grand opening in a couple of weeks, and trying to avoid both Will and Nina that she hadn't had an honest to God conversation with anyone during that same time period. And while her and Lucky's exchange didn't change or solve anything, it had allowed her to vent and the mere act of doing so made her feel enormously better.

Lucky shifted in her booth. ''So have you called Ginger to invite her to lunch yet?''

Renae shook her head, intrigued by the way Lucky had worded the question. She hadn't asked about her proposal, although, when they'd initially discussed it, she had offered to take a look at it if Renae wanted her to. ''I'm still putting the finishing touches on the documentation.''

Lucky seemed to be looking at her a little too closely.

Renae considered telling her about the other troublesome person in her life at that moment, but decided there was such a thing as too much venting. Especially to one person.

She got the ridiculous image of Lucky leaving the restaurant with her hair permanently blown back from her face from the impact of Renae's rants, and smiled inwardly.

''You know, you may just be using this whole hot dog versus filet mignon argument as a crutch to keep you from advancing your relationship with Will.''

It was Renae's turn to blink at her friend. ''What?''

Lucky shrugged, as if it were of no consequence to her, but Renae got the impression that Lucky was sharing more than advice. "Let's just say I've been there. And it's a constant topic of conversation between Colin and me." She put the last half of her hot dog down and brushed her hands on a paper napkin. "Sometimes I feel like I'm in so far over my head I just want to scream."

Renae realized she hadn't even blinked at the odd pairing of Colin the psychologist with one-time bar waitress Lucky. Which further emphasized the holes in her own argument.

"I mean, Colin took me to the opera at the Valentine Theatre a couple of weeks ago. The opera. I didn't have a clue how to dress, what to say when he introduced me to people he's known for years…." She swallowed hard, indicating she still wasn't completely over the experience. "Doing something like that is second nature to Colin but for me—"

"You'd take a smoke-filled bar any day."

Lucky smiled. "Yes. Something like that. Only they're not smoke-filled anymore, are they? What with the new law and all."

"Shame. I was thinking about taking up the habit."

Lucky smiled.

"Did Colin pick up on your feelings?"

"Of course. What kind of psychologist, and lover, would he be if he hadn't?"

"And I suppose he made you talk about it until you were blue in the face afterward." Renae shook her head. "I can't imagine what it would be like being involved with a shrink. I mean, does he have an off switch, or is he basically on all the time?"

Lucky smiled. "We're working on the off switch."

Renae sat for long moments merely enjoying being in Lucky's company. While the details of their past were different, she felt a connection with the other woman that she'd never felt with anyone else. Sure, she and Tabitha were close, but it had taken their friendship several years and many shared memories to be cultivated. In contrast, she and Lucky had clicked the first day Lucky had walked up to Women Only looking for a job.

At any rate, with very few words she knew Lucky would understand where she was coming from in just about any situation, and the same went for her with Lucky. Neither one of them was completely comfortable discussing her feelings. And that mere fact made it easier for both of them to do it.

"You know, it probably wouldn't be easy living with an E.R. surgeon, either."

Renae's gaze snapped to Lucky's face. She pretended an over-interest in dipping the last of her potato chips into the leftover chili topping, but Renae wasn't fooled.

"I mean, there's all that being on call. The long hours. The follow-ups during his down time."

"You seem to know an awful lot about E.R. docs," she said carefully.

Lucky's grin was infectious. "That's because I've been asking Colin a lot about them in case the information might come in handy."

"Hmm. Does he know about me and Will?"

She nodded. "Seems Will told him."

Renae's breath left her lungs. "Will told him?"

"That's what I said."

"What else did he say?" Renae felt ridiculously like she was in grade school talking about a guy she had a crush on.

Lucky shrugged. "I don't know."

"What do you mean you don't know?"

The restaurant owner came up to the table. Lucky greeted him.

"You know all that fast food is no good for you. You should let me give you something else next time. Something Greek, maybe," the Cypriot said with a friendly smile.

"Maybe."

"Okay, then. You girls have a nice day, no?"

"Yes," Lucky said.

"Eat here often?" Renae leaned forward. "What else did he say?"

Lucky looked momentarily confused, then she

backtracked to what they'd been talking about before the restaurant owner had come up. "I already told you, I don't know. Colin held up his hands and refused to say anything else, you know, while wearing that expression that said he was afraid he'd already said too much."

Renae chewed on that as a waitress took their plates away then gave them each a piece of pie, compliments of Frixos Stylianides.

She picked up her fork, toyed with the flaky top crust, then said, "Will and I are just like this piece of pie—"

Lucky held up a forkful of whipped cream. "Don't even start."

11

WILL STOOD BEHIND the partially closed vertical
blinds in his living room, watching as Renae parked
her Cadillac convertible in the lot. She had the top
down despite the heat, her sunglasses perched on
the edge of her straight nose, her dark blond hair
windblown and sexy, her skin glowing like warm
honey in the afternoon sun.

And damn if he didn't want her more now than
ever.

He dry-washed his face with his hands. His continued powerful attraction to her didn't make any
sense to him. Sure, ever since she'd moved in six
months ago, he'd had a thing for her, an intense
physical reaction, although it was restricted to his
fantasy life and at the time included her roommate,
Tabitha.

Then he'd slept with her.

Well, that sentence was sorely lacking, wasn't it?
He hadn't merely slept with her. He'd been lucky
if he'd gotten a straight four hours of sleep ever
since running into her by the mailboxes nearly a

week ago (had it really only been a week?). At first his lack of shut-eye had been the result of their having sex—constantly.

Now, however, his inability to saw some much-needed logs stemmed solely from his *not* having sex with her. If that made any sense. Which, of course, it didn't. Because nothing about his life made much sense of late.

Will watched as Renae went about taking grocery bags from the trunk then headed for the building without bothering to put the top up on her car. She wore a black tank that seemed to emphasize her deep tan, and white slacks that made him squint in case he could catch a glimpse of what she wore underneath. She looked good enough to eat and Will suddenly found himself ravenous.

She pushed her glasses to sit on top of her pretty head and looked up at his window. Will stepped slightly back, although he couldn't really say why. He grimaced as she moved out of sight, likely entering the building. Moments later he heard her footfalls on the steps in the hall. The rustling of her plastic grocery bags stopped just outside his door. Will waited. Would she knock?

He heard the rustling again then shortly thereafter the closing of her condo door upstairs.

Damn.

Behind him the telephone began ringing. He

stood for long moments, ignoring it, not up to another conversation with Janet should it happen to be her. But the caller was persistent and somewhere around the tenth ring he stepped into the dining room and picked up the extension.

''Willem?''

Relief suffused Will's muscles when he identified the caller as his mother. Though his name was William, she'd always left out a vowel and changed another.

''Hallo, Mum,'' he greeted, easily falling back to his native accent. Not that he made an effort otherwise, but his speech pattern naturally blended with those around him when he was in the States. ''How's everything?''

''Fine, fine. With you?''

Will paused. And the instant he did so, he knew he'd live to regret it. ''Fine. Couldn't be better.''

He cringed. Even worse, the overdoing it part.

''Mmm. That's interesting. Because judging from the sound of your voice, it's anything but. Come on. Be a dear and tell your ole mum what's happening in your life.''

Dorothy Sexton had five children, of which he was the middle child. He was the only one to leave England, and each of his siblings had not only stayed close by the family, they now had families of their own, including his youngest sister, Nancy, who had married last year and was due her first child any day now.

"Nothing much, you know. The same old, actually. Has Nancy dropped the bun yet?"

"Nancy's as big as an overstuffed sofa and just as uncomfortable. And quit trying to change the subject."

Will smiled as he sat down at the kitchen table.

Even though they were an ocean apart, and it was two in the afternoon by his watch and 7:00 p.m. in London, the clear sound of her voice made it seem like she was right next door. "It's nothing, really. Just some things happening at work."

"The doctor of the family is having problems, is he?"

While two of his siblings had pursued higher education, he was the only one to go as far as he had, mostly on scholarship and a mountain of student loans he'd just managed to pay off a year or so ago. While he was usually quite proud of what he'd accomplished, it never took more than a few words from his mother to remind him of his roots and his family and how he was still just the middle Sexton child from Southwark to her.

"You see, I've been after this promotion for some time now and I fear I may never achieve it."

He wouldn't go into detail about why. The whole Janet-Renae issue would only confuse her and he was half afraid she'd be on the next plane over if she thought that either of them might be wife material. Which was funny, because none of his family had come to visit him. As far as they were concerned, he was on the other side of the world, not a five-hour plane trip away.

Then again, he hadn't been home more than once a year for a week or two himself. And for some reason the thought suddenly made him sad.

"Hang in there, my boy. If there's one thing I know for sure in this world it's that whatever my Willem wants, my Willem gets."

He grinned at the familiar refrain, sometimes said in exasperation, most often with pride.

"Thanks, Mum. I guess I needed to hear that." He shifted in the chair. "So tell me, what did you have for dinner today?"

"It's Friday so we had shepherd's pie, of course. Your da's favorite."

Will closed his eyes, imagining the cramped Sexton kitchen with its old Formica table and red-plastic covered chairs, the room redolent with the smell of lamb and thick mashed potatoes. Of course, it would be only his mum and his da there now, the kids all gone, but two Sundays a month the whole family still gathered at the small flat for roast beef, Yorkshire pudding and two veg for dinner.

For the first time in his years in America, he genuinely missed home.

"If I recall correctly, shepherd's pie used to be your favorite, as well," his mother said. "But that's probably changed to a Burger Mac and, what do they call chips? Fries. Yes, fries, I think."

Will perked right up, as he suspected his mother knew he would. "On the contrary, I have fish 'n' chips for lunch nearly every other day. And I'll also have you know that I've been known to whip up quite a hotpot every now and again...."

And so it went, his mother challenging him on forgotten traditions and him defending himself. And for a short little while Will managed to forget about Renae and Janet and work and concentrated solely on his mother and everything he loved about her and England.

RENAE STOOD INSIDE her condo door and took a deep breath. Merely coming home anymore was awkward. She'd known Will was in his apartment, his behemoth of a SUV was parked right up front in the lot. Just knowing he was in the same building, that only a couple of doors separated them, sent her hormones into overdrive.

Or was it her hormones?

"There's someone I haven't seen much of lately."

Renae automatically smiled at Tabitha who had craned her neck from where she sat on the living-room couch to look at her.

"Hey."

"Hey, yourself. Why don't you go put that stuff away and come sit with me? I don't know about you, but I'm going into chat withdrawal."

It took Renae a whole two minutes to put the few items she'd picked up at the market away—milk, juice, eggs, a loaf of bread. She tucked the plastic bags into the recycling bin then grabbed a couple of sodas from the fridge and walked into the living room. The hideous pillows and throws aside, Tabitha had created a room that felt comfortable the instant you entered it. She sank down onto the faux suede couch beside her friend and handed her the other soda. Luckily Nina was nowhere in sight.

Tabby thanked her then said, "So tell me what's going on in Renae's world."

Renae stared at her. It seemed odd that so much had happened in such a short period of time. Or maybe it hadn't and she was making a big deal out of it.

She thought about the proposal she had tucked away for Women Only. It seemed strange that her best friend, the woman she shared a condo with, didn't know a thing about it.

"You still having sex with the sexy doc downstairs?"

Renae settled deeper into the cushions and crossed her legs. "No. That ended a couple of days ago."

After her and Lucky's conversation today at lunch, she found herself thinking of what her mother's reaction would be to the news that she was sleeping with a surgeon. No doubt, Daisy Truesdale would be overjoyed that her daughter had landed herself a doctor. Then again, she might not even bat an eye at the news. After all, the Truesdale women knew how to bag a man with deep pockets.

She shuddered.

"Wow, that must have been some thought."

Renae blinked Tabitha's face back into focus. "Sorry. I guess I'm not very good company today."

Tabitha leaned her arm against Renae's. "Who said you're good company at any other time?"

Renae smiled. "Our long-standing friendship, maybe?"

"Yes. I guess that would be proof."

They sat that way for long moments, neither of them saying anything as Renae reflected on the many years she'd known Tabitha. And how she might bring up her suspicions about Nina without alienating her friend and jeopardizing their friendship.

Tabitha toyed with the remote, turning down the sound as she settled on a soap opera. The great-looking guy and beyond beautiful girl on the screen loomed surreal and inaccessible to Renae.

"You know, I've always told you that men are more trouble than they're worth," Tabitha said.

Renae laughed. "My mood has nothing to do with Dr. Will."

"Sure it doesn't."

"Speaking of people being more trouble than they're worth, where's Nina?"

Tabitha jabbed her thumb in the direction of the hall. "In the bedroom."

"Oh. I thought maybe she wasn't here."

Her friend looked at her curiously. "You don't like her much, do you?"

Renae thought about how she might fill Tabby in on her missing notes and her messed-up cell phone and the items of clothing that she'd noticed had disappeared, but in the end she bit down hard on her bottom lip. Truth was, she hadn't liked Nina since first meeting her, and while the notes were a little hard to explain away, the rest of it was circumstantial so she feared she'd merely sound catty if she mentioned it.

She put her arm around Tabitha's shoulders. "What matters is that you like her."

"Mmm. And that I do."

They settled into the couch together, Renae's arm around Tabitha, their physical closeness mirroring their emotional connection.

"You know, she only has the best things to say about you," Tabitha said.

Renae nearly choked on her soft drink. "Excuse me?"

Tabby nodded. "She's always talking about how nice you are, how pretty, and how lucky I am to have you as a friend."

"Are you sure we're talking about the same person?"

"Yes."

"Funny, because whenever I'm in the same room with her the air conditioner isn't necessary."

Tabitha laughed. "It's just your imagination."

"No, it's not. It's plain fact. That girl doesn't like me, doesn't like our friendship, and I suspect if I said I was moving out she wouldn't hesitate to help me pack."

"You're being paranoid."

Was she? Renae was positive she wasn't.

"Why would she say such nice things about you to me, then?"

"Because she knows how you feel about me, more than likely. I mean if she were to slam me verbally, what would you do?"

Tabitha thought for a minute. "I don't know. A

month ago I would probably have asked her to leave.''

Renae searched her face. "And now?"

Her friend remained silent for longer than Renae was comfortable with. She'd sensed a change in the atmosphere for a while now. Watched as Tabitha grew more involved with Nina, their relationship deepening until Renae had begun feeling like a third, very unwanted wheel.

Now she had the proof that she was.

"What do you think of this one?"

Renae and Tabitha turned to where Nina had entered the room wearing a pink and white striped dress, looking more like Suzie Homemaker than Nina the Lesbian.

"Oh, hi, Renae. I didn't hear you come in."

"Hi, yourself." Renae shivered and pretended an interest in finishing off the contents of her can, sensing Tabitha's gaze on her.

"You didn't answer my question," Nina said in a whiny voice that turned Renae's shiver into a shudder. "Is this better than the last one?"

Tabitha tapped her finger against her lips as she considered her lover. She requested she turn around so she could see the back. "I think I like the first one better."

Nina blew out a long breath. "I like this one."

"So wear that one then."

"You are absolutely no help at all." She swung on her heels and headed back toward the bedroom where she lightly slammed the door.

"Hot date tonight?" Renae asked.

"Mmm. A couple of friends of ours are getting married. You remember Marty and Jo."

That would be Martha and Joann. "Sure, I do. Give them my congratulations, won't you?"

They heard slamming drawers and closet doors come from the other room as Renae settled back into the cushions and enjoyed her friend's company for as long as she had it.

"Talk about people being more trouble than they're worth," she said quietly.

She wasn't sure what Tabitha's response would be, but was grateful when she started laughing so hard Renae couldn't help but join in.

THAT SUNDAY NIGHT Will paced outside the doors of the Toledo Express Airport, wanting to be anywhere but there waiting for Janet to disembark from her plane. He spotted a couple of smokers standing near an ashtray and wished he'd taken up the habit, if only to have something to do with his hands right then.

Hell. Sheer hell. That was his life of late. And unfortunately he didn't see that changing anytime *soon*. Not when the girl he was dating, who had no idea Renae existed much less that he'd been sleeping with her, would be standing in front of him any moment.

Did he look different? Did his infidelity show on his face?

You can't be unfaithful if you're not having sex with her.

Renae's words came back to haunt him. Oh, yeah, that would sound good, wouldn't it? "Janet, honey, it didn't count."

"Will!"

He swiveled around at the same time Janet dropped her bags and threw herself into his arms.

Oh God in heaven, he was going to burn for this one.

He fought more to keep his balance than to return the enthusiastic hug. Had he ever been greeted so warmly by someone before? Even his mother made do with a dry peck to the cheek and a pat on the shoulder.

"God, you don't know how good it is to see you," she said.

He wished he could say the same but the truth was he'd been dreading this moment for so long that, now that it was here, he wanted to run flat-out in the opposite direction.

She finally loosened her grasp and stood back to smile up at him.

Pretty. She was still very pretty. Her soft brown hair was pulled back into an efficient ponytail, her makeup was simple and her polo shirt and cargo shorts looked very California.

"You look good enough to eat," she said.

Will started, trying not to recall that he'd thought the same words a mere five days ago—and that he hadn't thought them about Janet but about Renae.

"How was your trip?" he asked, bending to pick up her bags.

"Thanks. It was fine. Long, but fine. Not a free seat on the plane which is always uncomfortable, but it's all right now that it's over."

Will felt like his smile was so brittle his teeth might shatter. "I'm parked over here."

He led the way and she followed by his side.

Her laugh caught him up short. "Where's the fire?"

Will realized that he was walking fast enough to qualify for a marathon. He forced himself to slow his step.

"Boy, you must really be glad to see me."

Janet tucked her hand into his arm and he nearly jumped out of his skin.

She looked at him curiously.

"Sorry," he said. "I haven't been getting much sleep lately."

She took her hand away. "And I think I know why."

12

WILL NEARLY SWALLOWED his tongue whole at Janet's quiet statement.

"What?" he practically croaked.

She looked down at the pavement in front of them. "I said I think I know why you haven't been sleeping much lately. Daddy told me."

Will blinked at her, unable to connect the dots. Her father knew about him and Renae?

"He asked me not to say anything, but I couldn't help it." She smiled up at him. "Congratulations on being considered for a promotion."

Will's relief was so complete that he nearly dropped into a puddle right then and there.

"Oh, yes, that," he said, remembering exactly how much he had on the line here. And not liking it one bit. A rock and a hard place had nothing on what he felt caught between that minute.

He realized she was waiting for a response and said quickly, "It really is quite exciting, isn't it? My finally being considered for that promotion, I mean."

She laughed. "What did you think I meant?"

He shrugged as they finally reached his SUV in the short-term parking section of the airport. One step at a time. That's how he would take this. One step at a time.

And thankfully this step allowed him the freedom of not looking at her. Instead he popped the back door of the SUV and hauled her suitcases inside. "I hadn't the faintest idea what you were talking about."

Will closed the back door and opened the passenger's side. As he helped her up, he felt mercury line his stomach. Her bringing up his bid for promotion was just as disturbing as her accusing him of being a cad while she was away, now, wasn't it? After all, he suspected that his dating her was the sole reason he was being considered for the position at all. Her mentioning it served to remind him of that fact like a brick to his head.

He paused before getting in the driver's side of the car, trying to gather his wits about him. He'd half hoped that the instant he'd seen Janet, everything would have clicked into place. That he'd have remembered why he'd been so interested in her. Why he'd gone five long months without sex when he would never have gone one week without before.

Instead he felt like even a bigger mess than he'd been before.

He climbed into the car and started it, offering up a half-assed smile in her direction.

"So, how was the convention?" he asked, desperately trying to divert the conversation away from him and onto her.

"It was great. So many new techniques and pharmaceutical breakthroughs. I feel like my head is going to burst with all the new information...."

And there she went.

Will instantly relaxed into the buttery-soft leather seat, listening as Janet told him about the latest in cancer research and the other residents and doctors she'd met, and how she looked forward to going to the next convention. And somewhere around her saying something about being amazed by how much had happened since she'd finished med school, he allowed his mind to wander.

How had he not noticed before how much she chattered? Maybe because before it hadn't bothered him. It didn't bother him now, either, he hastened to point out. So he wasn't tuned in to every word she was saying. Surely that was the case with every relationship. You couldn't be "on" every minute of every day. It was unreasonable even to think it.

She's only been back for ten minutes, a small voice in his head said.

Oh, shut up, he told it.

"Did you say something?"

Will blinked several times then looked at Janet. "No, no. Not a word." He tried his best grin. "Please continue. It makes me wish I had gone with you."

Oh, boy, did he ever wish he'd gone to the convention with her. If he had, he wouldn't be marinating in the duck soup he currently sat in the middle of.

She tapped the soft-sided briefcase on the floor next to her feet. "Don't worry. I took plenty of notes for you."

Had he just winced?

Yes, he had.

Of course he had. Because the more Janet talked, the lower he felt. She'd taken notes for him. How thoughtful.

How anal.

His brows shot up on his forehead.

He was getting the very definite impression that there was a war of sorts being played out on the battlefield of his subconscious. But why and from which direction the shots were being fired, he couldn't be sure. And until he found out, he had the sinking sensation he was going to be a mere bystander.

He merged with traffic in the right-hand lane of Airport Highway, hating that the airport was so far from the city. A half hour drive sitting in the hot seat before he could drop Janet off.

A half hour of sheer hell.

He grew aware of Janet's silence next to him and looked over to find her staring out the window. It almost looked as if she were thinking the same thing he was. Which was ridiculous, really. He was merely projecting his emotions onto her.

He cleared his throat. "So, how is L.A., anyway? I've never been, myself."

She glanced at him. "Actually I didn't get much of a sense of the city. There was a tour bus that took us to Anaheim one day, but I met this wonderful resident from Minnesota and she and I talked throughout the entire trip. I can't even remember the color of the bus."

She'd gone to L.A. and hadn't seen any of the city. No Rodeo Drive, no Grauman's Chinese Theatre. How dedicated.

How boring.

Will tightened his grip on the steering wheel.

"It seemed nice enough. Smoggy. Different. In fact, while I…"

Off she went again. Which, Will firmly told himself, was a far sight better than her silence moments ago. So long as she was talking, everything was all right. He wasn't looking at her too closely. And, more important, she wasn't looking at him too closely.

Finally, in the middle of Janet's description of the hotel she'd stayed in and the convention layout, he pulled up in front of her apartment complex in Sylvania, on the western edge of Toledo. He gazed at the new buildings as if they were the Promised Land.

"Well, here we are," he proclaimed unnecessarily.

Janet looked around her. "Oh! I didn't even register that we were here already."

Will, on the other hand, had mentally been there for the past thirty minutes.

He shut off the engine and climbed out, meeting Janet at the back of the SUV.

He jumped when Janet tucked her hand into his arm as they walked to her building. "You know, I've had a lot of time to think while I've been away," she said.

"Oh?" Will was busy counting the steps left to the door. Thirty, twenty-nine…

"Mmm-hmm."

The tone of her voice snapped his head around even as he quickened his steps.

"I was thinking—"

Will swung the building door open so fast he nearly hit her head-on with it.

"Oh!"

"Sorry," he mumbled. "Are you all right?"

She'd put a hand to her chest then checked out the status of her ponytail…complete with pink ribbon.

Damn him and his childhood obsession with girls in ribbons. Especially shiny pink ones.

"Here, why don't you give me your keys?" he said as they ascended the steps to her second-floor apartment.

She handed him her keys, complete with pompom key chain in blue and gold. The reminder that she'd been a football cheerleader jolted him a bit.

"There you go," he said, swinging open her apartment door—thankfully it opened in so there was no risk of bodily harm—and putting her suitcases down inside the door without actually entering. "Home safe and sound."

She hadn't said anything and Will realized that he hadn't really looked at her since midway through their drive from the airport.

He looked at her now and was fairly convinced he'd just swallowed his tongue.

"You know, you haven't kissed me yet," she said in a low voice he had once viewed as sultry.

She hooked her finger inside the flap and between the middle buttons of his oxford shirt.

Oh, boy.

"Sure, I did," he croaked.

Hadn't he?

She shook her head. "Which brings me back to what I thought about when I was in L.A."

Oh, God. She had that look on her face. Not one he'd seen her wear before, but the expression he'd seen on countless women's faces—had seen on Renae's face more times than he could count—right before they were going to make an indecent proposal.

"All this...waiting until my wedding night stuff..." She edged closer to him, but rather than making him hot, it made him want to edge farther away from her. "Well, I've decided it's old-fashioned."

Will swallowed hard, incapable of making a response. Not because he was turned on beyond belief, but because he was occupied with measuring the maneuver it would take him to make it to the stairs.

"I want you, Will," Janet whispered, kissing his chin and smiling up into his eyes. "I want you now. Tonight."

"Sex?" Will blurted.

She gave a quiet giggle. "Yes, sex."

Oh, boy, oh, boy, oh boy...

Janet dislodged her finger from between his buttons and curved her hands around his waist until she had her fingers flat against his rear end. He gave a startled sound of disbelief.

Was this the same woman who for five months had waited for him to make the first move? Who had said no to him so many times that he'd begun to think he'd just have to marry her to get her out of her panties?

A little over a week ago he'd said goodbye to a docile lamb. Now he was facing a she-cat intent on getting what she wanted.

Janet rubbed herself suggestively against his front.

Strangely enough, Big Ben didn't budge.

"Make love to me, Will," Janet breathed, moving even closer to kiss him.

The moment before her mouth would make contact with his, he caught her shoulders and jerked her away. She gasped, nearly losing her balance and falling backward into her apartment. She probably would have had he not had a vise grip on her shoulders. Not to keep her from falling, but to keep her away.

"Actually I've been doing…some thinking of my own while you've been away," he said, his words coming quickly, a trickle of sweat working its way down his forehead. "And I don't happen to think waiting for one's wedding night is old-fashioned at all." He tried for a grin but was afraid he'd ended up with a grimace. "In fact, I was just telling Colin that your impressive self-control and need for tradition are what initially attracted me to you."

Even as he spoke, he stepped backward, his reach growing longer as he continued to hold her at bay.

"And it's what continues to attract me to you...."

Just two more steps but he couldn't make them without letting her go first.

"In fact, I think I should go before we do something we both might regret."

"Will!"

He was about to release her but instead held tight. "What?"

"You haven't even kissed me yet."

"Oh, yes. Right."

With his feet planted at the top of the stairs, he leaned in, hesitated at the look of submission on her face as she tilted up her chin, then he gave her what had to be the driest, quickest peck on the cheek in history.

"Very well, then. Good night!"

And with that he was down the stairs and out of the building like a shot.

13

RENAE SAT ON THE STEPS outside the condo door, listening as Tabitha and Nina had one of their world-famous arguments. Actually it was more like a fanatical rant. Essentially Tabitha tried to reason with Nina while her irate lover raged on for what sometimes seemed like hours.

Renae stared down longingly at the half gallon of Ben & Jerry's Chunky Monkey she'd run out to get.

The agreement she and Tabitha had come to when Renae had moved in was that if there was a heated situation with one or the other of them with their significant others, they would make themselves scarce.

In this case it meant that rather than going inside and interrupting the scene that was undoubtedly taking place in the living room, Renae was sitting on the hall steps with a carton of melting ice cream, without a spoon. Which seemed to pretty much sum up the whole of her life at that very moment.

She parked her elbows on her knees then dropped

her head into her hands. Was it really just over a week ago that everything had been running like clockwork? When she'd been happy with her job at Women Only without yearning for more? When she'd come home with no suspicion of someone sabotaging her personal belongings and tampering with her cell phone? When she'd been happily single without thoughts of a hunky, unavailable surgeon hanging out on the fringes of her mind—whether she was awake or asleep—always present, always tempting her?

Yep, her life was a carton of melting ice cream without a spoon and she wasn't sure what, if anything, she could do with the mess that would surely remain afterward.

And there would be an afterward, wouldn't there?

She puzzled over that one.

If there was one thing life had taught her it was that there was always an afterward. Postchildhood. Postadolescence. Hell, there was even postpartum depression, although she hoped never to run into that one. Then again, judging by the way her life was progressing so far, she'd probably have to suffer through that as well when and if she ever got married and had children.

Now there was a thought….

Her cell phone vibrated in her pocket. She sighed as she fished it out, then stared at the lighted display. Her mother. Oh, great. Just what she needed now.

"Hi, Mom."

"God, I hate caller ID," Daisy Truesdale said with a dramatic sigh. "You can never surprise anyone anymore."

"You never surprise me anyway." Simply because her mother's goal in life was to provide constant surprises, so Renae had come to expect them. "What's up?"

"Why does anything have to be up in order for me to call my daughter, my only child?"

If there was any justice in this world, it was that Daisy had only had one child to screw up. "Because something's always up."

Renae was aware she was being more cynical than usual. Probably had something to do with being locked out of her own apartment while sitting on the steps watching her favorite ice cream melt.

"Okay, in this case, you're right."

Renae closed her eyes, mentally bracing herself.

"I'm moving to Vegas to become a showgirl."

Renae shook her head and grimaced. Her mom, a forty-three-year-old Vegas showgirl. At least it was in line with the remainder of Daisy Truesdale's life. Underage stripper at seventeen who'd gotten pregnant by a customer who'd sworn he'd always take care of her then had burned rubber when he'd found out she was pregnant. Renae had been raised in the back rooms of strip clubs around pasties and G-strings and silicone breasts. And as soon as she was old enough, she'd followed in her mother's footsteps, never really knowing any other kind of life.

Until Ginger.

"So?" her mother said after long moments. "Are you going to say anything?"

"What's there to say?"

"I don't know. Good luck?"

"Good luck."

"Well, that sounded sincere."

Renae's shoulders slumped. She didn't mean to be rude to her mom, she really didn't. It was just that so much of her life was for crap right now that she couldn't sum up much enthusiasm for Daisy's latest escapade. From dancing on cruise ships, going to New York to try her hand at Broadway, this new news wasn't...well, new.

"Look, Mom, are you leaving today?"

"No. Not for another week."

"Good then, we have some time. I've really got to go right now, though."

A few moments later, after promising Daisy she would call by tomorrow, Renae disconnected the call and turned off her phone, resisting the urge to lie back on the floor in a gesture of surrender. She didn't know if anyone was currently controlling the strings of her life, but if they were, she wanted to write them a long, detailed letter of complaint.

Downstairs, she heard the outer door open. She sat up a little straighter, hoping it wasn't anyone who lived on the third floor who might see her sitting outside. Nudging the bag of ice cream aside with her foot, she bent over to look down the stairwell. She made a strangled sound as Will looked right up to stare into her eyes.

And the day just kept getting better and better.

She supposed that's what she got for questioning the great puppeteer of life.

Renae quickly drew back and closed her eyes. Oh, great. What she really needed right now was for Will to think she was sitting there waiting for him.

Her heart thudded against her rib cage as she strained to hear him continue up the stairs to his apartment. Nothing. Which was a good thing, right? Because it meant he wasn't coming up—

Something touched her arm. She shrieked and nearly leapt straight out of her skin.

"Whoa. I mean, I know I have quite an impact on the ladies, but I didn't think I was that good."

Renae stared into Will's face, but rather than finding the grin that normally would have accompanied his words, he wore a grimace. A handsome, irresistible grimace that made her stomach pitch to somewhere in the vicinity of her feet and made her toes curl where they were visible in her flip-flops.

Toes he seemed to be a little preoccupied with presently.

"Um, hi," she said. "In case you're wondering, I'm not sitting here waiting for you."

As if on cue, the sound of something breaking against the apartment door made them both jump, indicating the argument within was not only still going strong, but had escalated.

Will looked from the door to her. "Actually I was going to ask if you'd forgotten your keys."

She held them up and again he seemed inordinately preoccupied with the simple silver icon of her astrological sign of Leo.

Renae tucked the keys half into her pocket, far enough to keep them anchored, then picked up the bag holding the ice cream.

What did he want? Surely he didn't expect her to buy that he'd been concerned she'd gotten locked out of her condo? Excuse her if she was wrong, but over the past few days she'd gotten the impression that if she'd been lying half dead in need of CPR, he'd have stepped over her and closed his condo door in order to avoid her.

She looked at him again, noticing how nice he looked in the simple white oxford shirt and tan

Dockers. All the tennis he played had given him a deep, golden tan, and kissed his forever-tousled hair with sun-bright highlights.

And when he grinned...

She swallowed hard as he did just that, the gesture seeming to call a halt to all rational thought and beckon to her body.

"Your ice cream's melting."

That's not all that was melting, but she wasn't about to tell him that. Especially not when she was getting freezer burn on her fingers from desperately holding the bag in front of her.

"Would you like a spoon?" he asked.

She'd like much more than a spoon from him. She wanted to follow him back to his place, shut off the air-conditioning and throw open the windows and see what imaginative things they could do with the ice cream to keep cool.

She must have looked suspicious because he sighed and looked away. "Hey, I'm not trying to come on to you. Trust me that's, um, the furthest thing from my mind right now." He ran his fingers through his hair. "I just thought that if you wanted to wait at my place, you know, until you can get back into your own, you're more than welcome."

Renae squinted at him. "Wait. At your place."

He nodded.

"Just...wait. Nothing more?"

"Nothing more. Well, unless you want to talk or something while you wait."

"Talk..." she said drawing out the word.

"Right. Bad idea."

Something else broke against the door. Renae stared at it. "That's going to leave a mark." She looked back at Will. "I think I'll take you up on your offer."

FIFTEEN MINUTES LATER Will was ready to have himself committed to the nearest mental health facility. Renae sat cross-legged on his leather sofa, the carton of ice cream in her lap, a spoon in one hand, the remote control in the other. She wore a baggy white sweat suit that had Women Only written across the chest in navy-blue cursive letters, she didn't have on a lick of makeup that he could tell, and her hair was pulled back into what he'd describe as a messy ponytail, with dark blond tendrils curving all over the back of her golden neck. Definitely not the type of ponytail he was usually drawn to. And nowhere was there a pink ribbon, or a ribbon of any color for that matter.

She found a station she liked and put the remote down on the coffee table.

"Are you sure you don't mind my waiting here?" she asked, glancing at him where he stood in the archway between living and dining room.

"I don't mind."

"It might be awhile."

Bugger. "That's fine."

"Do you like *Sex and the City?*"

Will nearly choked on his own saliva.

Renae didn't miss his reaction if her own momentary pause was any indication. And he'd bet the Queen's royal jewels that it was.

She pointed at the television and he realized she was talking about the show.

Not that it mattered. The idea of watching the provocative sitcom while in the same room as her was a bad one, no matter which way you sliced it.

She appeared to feel the same as she reached for the remote with a trembling hand and switched the channel to a news show.

Better, but only slightly.

He glanced into the kitchen behind him. "I'm, um, just going to make myself something to eat. Do you want anything?"

She lifted the carton of ice cream without looking at him.

"Right."

She'd offered him some of the cold concoction when he'd originally handed her a spoon, but he thought it better if he passed, especially considering the way she put the spoon first into her mouth to wet it before sticking it into the carton. Renae's licking anything was not something he thought he should be watching now.

He stood with the refrigerator door open for long minutes. He didn't get it. Not a half hour ago he'd had a beautiful woman he'd been lusting after for the past five months practically throwing herself at him and he'd run from her like a bat out of hell. While now...

He began taking items out of the refrigerator without looking at them. He'd figure it all out on the counter. Something, anything, to take his mind off the sexier-than-sin woman sitting in the other room. She laughed at something and Will dropped a green pepper.

The initial plan had been to pick Janet up from the airport, take her to dinner, then drive her home, so he hadn't had anything to eat since a bagel that had served as breakfast-lunch. The problem was, his appetite didn't seem interested in anything he looked at. He went through the cupboards, coming away with the same feeling.

Great. He needed something to do while Renae was inside his apartment, something to keep his hands busy if not his mind, and he couldn't seem to produce a single, solitary idea as to what.

Scooping the food items back up, he dumped them into the refrigerator then closed the door.

Okay, that had burned up an entire thirty seconds.

He turned around and found himself staring at Renae where she stood in the doorway.

Damn.

Damn, damn, damn.

Up this close, in the bright, unflattering light of the kitchen, she looked even better. Her green eyes were a mesmerizing, creamy jade, her skin was clean and inviting, her body soft and tempting even with all that thick cloth on top of it.

"Aren't you...um, hot?" he asked, motioning toward the heavy material and long sleeves.

She either misinterpreted his meaning, or purposely chose to ignore it. "Very."

Will's willpower was quickly deserting him. His palms itched to feel her skin. His very skin seemed to yearn to touch hers.

"This helps," she said, holding out the closed carton of ice cream in front of him.

"I'm not a big fan of ice cream."

"Try it. You might like it."

Will was through with trying things he wasn't supposed to like.

"Then could you hold it in your freezer for me until I can get back into my place?"

"Oh, um, sure."

He took the carton and put it away. When he turned back around, she was on his other side. Not only was she on his other side, she was bending over, her perfectly rounded rump high in the air as she gained access to his dishwasher.

She backed up in order to close the door, putting that same delectable rump in direct contact with Big Ben, who had definitely had a change of heart since dropping Janet off.

"Oh!" Renae swung to face him, her skin wonderfully flushed, mussed tendrils of hair clinging to her cheek. Will caught her by the shoulders to prevent her from falling backward. "I was just, um, putting the spoon in the dishwasher."

"I see that."

"Of course."

Will found it ironic that he was holding Renae in the exact same manner he'd been holding Janet such a short time ago. But rather than using the grip to hold Renae away from him, he was battling with the most incredible desire to pull her closer.

His gaze swept over her features. From her remarkable eyes, to her softly feathered brows, her high forehead and cheekbones, down her smooth jawline to her downright wicked mouth.

Her pink, pink tongue darted out to moisten her lips and fire raged a path down his stomach straight to his groin.

And confusion reigned in his head.

He didn't get it. What was it about this one woman that he couldn't seem to stop wanting her?

Couldn't seem to stop thinking about her? The only common bond they shared was sex. They talked about nothing else, did nothing else.

Then why was it that when Dr. Stuart Nealon had told him about his possible promotion the other night, it had been Renae he'd wanted to share the news with? Not only hadn't he thought of telling Janet, he hadn't even felt inclined to discuss it with her when she'd brought it up. Why was it Renae was the first thing he thought about every morning when he woke up, and was the last thing he thought about before he went to sleep?

Why was it he wanted this woman with an intensity that scared the hell out of him?

"Here," she said, her voice low and gravelly. "Let me make this easier on you."

Then she was kissing him, and he was more than letting her—he was kissing her back. And every coherent thought scattered from his mind as he gave himself over to sensation.

14

RENAE FELT as if she'd been trapped in an airless room for the past four days and that she was just now being allowed to take in a long, fresh breath.

Will's mouth on hers felt so damn good. So right.

The hands that had been on her shoulders moments before now gently cupped her jaw, holding her still as he slowly leaned his head one way and kissed her, then the other, his lips softly massaging hers. Renae's bones melted and she sought support from him. Had she ever been kissed so sweetly? So honestly? So tenderly? She couldn't remember. But what she did know was that she'd never been kissed that way by Will before. And she wasn't sure what to do with this change in him.

His fingers moved from her jaw to her neck, then over her shoulders until his hands finally rested against her bottom. She gasped when he hiked her up to sit on the counter, his mouth barely breaking from its sweet, torturous attentions.

Renae shifted to a more comfortable position on the hard granite then wrapped her calves around his waist, pulling him in until his long, hard sex rested solidly against hers through their clothing. A shiver started somewhere in the vicinity of her toes then spread up and up and up until it was a downright shudder by the time it reached her shoulder blades. Will's fingers found the hem of her sweatshirt and pushed it up, then pressed against her quivering stomach.

Will broke briefly from their kiss and stared deep into her eyes. Renae was helpless to do anything but stare back. He seemed puzzled, as if he was trying to figure something out. In the back of her mind she told him not to bother. That she'd been doing the same thing since the day she'd first given in to her temptation for him and she'd finally accepted that there was no explanation for what she felt for him. It merely…was.

Then he was kissing her again.

Renae moaned as he unsnapped her bra then stroked her breasts under the soft material. Each of his moves was so slow, so meaningful that she didn't know how to respond, how to react. He tugged the sweatshirt up and over her head then slipped her bra free, both items of clothing hitting the floor at his feet.

''You *are* hot.''

Will's quiet words seemed to caress her along with his breath. He drew a finger down the damp skin between her breasts, then slid it inside the waistband of her pants. Renae braced herself against the side of the counter as he stripped the cotton from her burning body, leaving the white lace of her panties in place. He moved away from her and she whimpered in protest.

Moments later he was opening the top of the ice-cream carton and retrieving a fresh spoon from a nearby drawer. For a moment she was afraid he might leave her like that, panting, nearly naked on the counter, as he went off to eat ice cream.

Until he spooned a healthy portion of the sweet concoction from the carton then held the dripping spoon above her right nipple.

Renae gasped, both surprised by his bold move and the cold sensation of the ice cream against her skin. She watched as the white ball started sliding down over her nipple. Will leaned in and caught it in his mouth, then licked her puckered flesh with long, slow stokes.

Her eyes drifted closed at the exquisite combination of hot and cold, inanimate and animate coming together on her right breast. Will finished laving her then drew her nipple deep into his mouth, seeming to pull on a line that went straight down to her clit.

He stepped away again and it was all Renae could do not to melt to the floor in front of him in a mindless puddle. She watched as he duplicated the ice-cream bit with her left nipple, this time allowing the cream to melt further until it pooled in her navel. By the time his tongue lapped around her belly ring, her elbows were trembling so badly she nearly couldn't hold herself upright.

"I…I thought you weren't an ice-cream kind of guy," she whispered so quietly she almost didn't hear herself.

His blue-eyed gaze met hers. "Lately I'm coming to realize that there's a lot about myself I don't understand."

Renae could not only relate to his statement, but she could empathize with Will. Ever since they'd taken things from flirty to dirty her life hadn't been the same. She was no longer content to just bring home a check from Women Only…couldn't ignore the goings-on in her own condo. And Will…

He pressed his mouth against the white cotton crotch of her panties and blew, nearly shooting her physically off the counter, and psychologically into another dimension.

Sex between them before had been about instant gratification, of seeking an orgasm, then seeking it all over again. They hadn't taken much time to explore each other at leisure. Any rest time had been reserved solely for rest. There'd been no foreplay, no during play, just "get down to the act, thank you very much" play.

His unhurried attention made a completely different kind of chaos accumulate in her belly. It was deeper, somehow, more intense, her heart thudding in a way that would have been scary had she been thinking clearly. Her hips automatically bucked up off the counter as he bared her to his gaze then fastened his lips firmly to her clitoris. Then again, how could she think clearly when he was doing his best to chase all coherent thought from her mind, period?

Will laved and suckled her with a patience and a consideration she'd never experienced before. His long tongue lapped her, meeting with the fleshy hood of her arousal then gently pulling it up until she trembled violently.

The world exploded behind Renae's closed eyelids, her hips jerking, her breathing ragged, but rather than freeing her, Will remained where he was, drawing out her crisis by suckling her, pulling the bud of her center into his mouth and swirling his tongue against it.

Renae ran her hands through his hair again and again, not wanting the moment to end, yet eager to have him connect with her in an even more intimate way.

As her climax ebbed, she tugged on the coarse

strands of his hair until he was once again kissing her. She devoured his mouth much as he had devoured hers moments before, somehow unable to get enough of him. Of the taste of herself on him. She restlessly pulled the hem of his oxford shirt from the waist of his slacks, surprised to find him still fully dressed. Rather than wasting time with all the buttons, she undid the first two then yanked the shirt over his head, barely pausing to let the piece of clothing fall to the floor before diving for the zipper to his slacks.

Will caught her hands in his and broke off the kiss.

Renae knew a moment of panic. Maybe there was a reason why he was still dressed. Maybe he didn't want her.

He leaned his forehead against hers and stared deep into her eyes for long moments. She heard her own deep swallow, words out of her reach. Then he grinned.

"Where's the fire, Renae?"

She wanted to tell him it was everywhere. Running rampant over her skin. Searing through her veins. Causing an inferno between her legs. But she didn't get the chance because as she watched, he slid her panties down her legs then opened his own slacks so that their clothes covered the kitchen floor.

Finally he was naked in front of her.

Renae shivered just looking at his fine masculine form. He was made up of just the right amount of muscle, lean and powerful and so mouthwateringly gorgeous he took her breath away. His skin was golden-brown from doing laps in the pool, the white swatch below his hips down to the tops of his legs like a welcoming beacon. This man and she were different in so many ways, she sometimes wondered how they'd ever come together. He exercised, she sunbathed. He oozed self-discipline and plowed ahead with single-minded intent while up until now she'd bounced off the walls of life, pondering each cut and bruise, unprepared when the next wall went up in front of her.

So different…but in that moment, the same.

She curved her calves around his legs and moaned when his rock-hard length was cradled in her soft, wet folds. He moved away to put on a condom he'd taken from his back pocket, and she watched, entranced, as the latex stretched across his straining member. Then she scooted closer to the edge of the counter so he would have easy access.

He fitted the tip of his erection against her fleshy portal and paused. Renae wanted to groan with impatience, force his entrance. Just when she might have reached down to do just that, he tilted his hips forward, entering her a scant few inches, then withdrawing.

Renae did moan. Too little…too fast.

Restless chaos built and built, her position of no power driving her insane. If they were in bed, she would have slammed him back to the mattress and then saddled and straddled him in two seconds flat.

He stroked her again and she tried to force him in to the hilt. He grasped her hips and held her still, withdrawing again.

Renae's breath came in such ragged gasps she actually heard herself. She wanted him to fill her so badly she throbbed with the power of her need, trembled, her body no longer her own, but his to do with as he pleased.

She frantically searched his face, finding his jaw tense, his expression determined as he entered her again, no doubt intent on withdrawing before hitting all the way home. But as she watched, the pure sensation of it seemed to wash over his face and instead of withdrawing, he was sliding into the hilt, finally filling her in the way she longed to be filled.

Every molecule of air exited from Renae's lungs. Every muscle contracted. She knew a moment of fear that she might not be able to breathe or move again. Then Will pulled slightly out and surged forward again, drawing a moan from her that broke the spell and coaxed her to an even higher plane of pleasure. The cool counter under her bottom was no longer hard. The kitchen itself no longer existed. All she knew was that moment and this man. And somewhere deep down she thought that's all that she really needed.

She tightened her legs around Will's hips, teetering on the edge of orgasm. Seeming to sense her condition, Will lengthened his strokes, each one a little faster than the one before. Renae stiffened as an almost unbearable pressure took hold of her stomach. She tightly gripped his shoulders, subconsciously trying to maintain balance even as she snowboarded off the edge and into a snow-white wilderness.

Somewhere through the clouds of her own climax, she heard Will's low groan, felt him go whipcord straight.

Long moments later they were out of breath and clinging to each other, sweat glistening on their bodies, the ice cream melting on the counter next to them. And Renae looked at Will as if she really didn't know him at all.

The sound of a ringing phone pierced her ears. Renae was reminded of another telephone call a few days earlier that had not only shattered the moment, but splintered her from Will. Was it going to happen again?

Will didn't want to acknowledge the ringing phone. Didn't want to withdraw from Renae's soft body. He wanted to explore the myriad emotions that once he'd relaxed and opened the gate to, had rushed through him like dam waters being set free.

He searched Renae's face and eyes. When he'd looked at her before tonight, he'd seen a sexy woman he couldn't wait to heat up the sheets with. Now...

Damn the ringing phone.

"I...think I should get that."

He watched as Renae dropped her gaze, looking everywhere but at him as he moved away from her. Two steps and he was snatching up the receiver in the dining room. "Sexton."

"Will? Is that you?"

He tried to place the female voice but couldn't. "This is he."

A sigh then, "Good. This is Tabitha, you know, Renae's roommate upstairs. She wouldn't happen to be with you, would she? I've been calling her cell but she's not picking up."

Will looked at where Renae had her back to him. She'd already put her panties and pants back on and was working on the sweatshirt, although he knew she had to be steaming hot in the heavy cotton.

"It's for you," he said, holding out the phone.

Renae turned to face him, her shocked expression touching something deep inside him.

"It's Tabitha," he explained.

She instantly appeared to relax as she took the

receiver then walked into the other room. Will used the time to clean up and get dressed himself. When Renae turned back around, he was leaning against the counter watching her.

"Coast is clear," she said, hanging the receiver back up.

Will nodded, feeling he should say something, wanting to say something, but unsure what exactly it was. He knew now wasn't the moment to lay on the table that, wrong or right, he no longer wanted to be with Janet.

After all, where did that leave him with Renae?

"Well, um, thanks for letting me wait here," she said, turning from him.

He followed her into the living room where she gathered her cell phone and her keys from the coffee table, then to the door where she appeared to hesitate for a moment before she closed it behind her.

Will leaned against the wood and dry-washed his face, trying to interpret everything that had happened in the past hour. More than just the sex. What had made him go to her when he'd seen her sitting on the stairs? What had compelled her to agree to wait at his place?

What had made him kiss her in the way he had?

He'd lived a fairly straightforward life. He'd grown up in South London in the working-class area of Southwark. No, he hadn't had the best clothes or the best bike or even the best education, but he'd made do with what he did have, getting strength from his parents whose work ethic was nothing if not stoic. Then he'd come to the States to attend medical school, bringing his sense of what he wanted out of life with him.

Or rather what he'd thought he'd wanted out of life.

Now everything emerged a thick, impenetrable fog, the future unclear and a tad intimidating.

He found himself absently rubbing his chest and looked down at where his heart still throbbed thickly beneath his breastplate. He'd never felt quite this way before, so he had absolutely no frame of reference to compare it to. To say, oh yes, I remember this, and shortly thereafter this, this and that would happen.

Instead he felt like he'd been flung into a vast sea and was navigating the waters without the aid of a chart or even a compass, the shore so far away as to be nonexistent.

The question was, did he allow the current to take him where it willed? Or did he pick up a paddle and make for the closest coast and familiar ground?

Now that was certainly something to think about....

15

RENAE NORMALLY DIDN'T have a problem with Monday mornings. But today…well, she suspected today would go down as her own personal worst. And it was only eleven o'clock. Not even the memory of last night, of her and Will, helped. In fact, considering what had happened since then, it actually hurt.

It hadn't been enough that her alarm hadn't gone off and she'd gotten up late. She hadn't been able to find the clean basket of laundry she'd put just inside her bedroom door the night before and had been forced to look for her belly-dancer costume. But when she'd put that on, an important thread had given across her breasts and the sequins had popped from the material like a series of buttons being ripped from a shirt. She'd had little doubt who had been behind the mishap, but she hadn't had the time to confront Nina as she'd rushed from the apartment in a bathing-suit top and belly-dancer bottoms, reaching Women Only with only ten minutes left to go into the class she'd been scheduled to lead.

Thankfully Lucky had stopped by the shop first thing and had not only opened, she had directed the class in her jeans and T-shirt. Renae had checked her cell phone to discover it had been switched off, something she didn't remember doing. In fact, after Tabitha had been forced to call Will's direct line, she distinctly remembered turning her cell back on before returning to her condo.

And now, two hours later, she was in the middle of her sixth interview from hell to fill the position that would be left open by Lucky's pending departure.

"I don't know how my mom would feel about my selling stuff...like this dildo," the fresh-faced nineteen-year-old woman said, picking up an electric massager and staring at it.

Renae wanted to tell the overgrown teen that maybe she should consider growing up and moving out of her parents' house. "I understand completely. I wouldn't want you selling anything you hadn't a clue about, either. This," she said, taking the box from her, "is a massager or a clitoris vibrator, not a dildo. And besides, one of the job requirements is that you not only know your physical self, but that you're an expert on it, you know, should you need to fill in for someone during our popular Clit 101 course."

The teen gasped, turned as red as the curtain to

the room where the class in question was conducted, then mumbled an apology as she headed for the door.

Lucky's laugh sounded from the counter where she was comparing inventory sheets. "Don't you think you were a little hard on her?"

Renae gave an eye roll. "Jesus, the girl probably didn't even know where her clitoris was."

"Yes, but when did that become one of the requirements for employment? I mean, a floor salesperson doesn't need to be an expert on the female anatomy."

Renae waved the massager. "No, but she should know that if a woman attempted to insert this she'd probably never get it back out." She shook her head as she restocked the item. "I can see the headlines now: 'The victim of electrocution was told she'd achieve the ultimate orgasm by a worker at Women Only.' And never mind the lawsuits."

Lucky tsked tsked. "Somebody woke up on the wrong side of the bed this morning." She tucked the inventory sheets away. "Actually, lately I've been wondering if you pushed your mattress against the wall so that you're getting up on the wrong side every morning."

Renae grimaced, then drew a deep breath and released it. "You're right. I have been a bit bitchy lately, haven't I?"

Lucky rounded the counter and came to stand in front of her. "Have you spoken to Ginger yet?"

Renae nodded. "Yeah. She can't have lunch with me until later this week."

Lucky smiled. "Well, that's good, isn't it? At least you'll finally get your proposal heard."

"Yeah, I guess. It's just that I couldn't help feeling she was giving me the brush-off. And, trust me, that's not a way I'm used to feeling with Ginger."

"I think she just has other things on her mind."

"Mmm." As did she.

Namely the person she'd seen coming out of Will's apartment this morning.

Lucky was looking at her a little too closely. "Are you sure that's all that's bothering you?"

"Yes," she said quickly. Then she leaned against the counter and sighed more than said, "No."

"Ah. I didn't think so."

"What is that supposed to mean?"

"That's supposed to mean that Colin told me the resident returned from California last night."

"Like I needed to be told that. I saw her coming out of Will's apartment at nine o'clock this morning."

The words were out before she could swallow them back.

Renae winced and turned toward the counter, going through a small pile of coupons then straightening and putting them back near the register for customers to take.

After last night, she hadn't known what she'd expected. She'd sensed that something had changed in Will…had changed in their strange relationship. But when she'd returned to her condo to find a momentary peace treaty had been signed by Tabitha and Nina, she'd determined to just let whatever was happening happen. It wasn't like she had any control over it anyway. The harder she tried to understand, the more elusive the answer became. She hoped coasting and allowing the road to take her where it may might shine a spotlight on what she was missing.

Upon coming to that conclusion, she had felt like the weight of the world had been lifted from her shoulders and had slept better that night than she'd slept in a long, long time. So well she was grinning when she'd awakened, even though her alarm hadn't gone off and she was late. Not even her missing clothing and her costume mishap had managed to wipe the smile from her face.

So there she was, wearing her bikini top and belly-dancer bottoms, taking Will a couple of bagels smothered with cream cheese and smoked salmon despite how late she was running, when she saw his condo door open…

And the resident come out.

She couldn't have been more shocked had someone scooped her up while sleeping and dumped her into an ice-cold pool.

And if all that hadn't been bad enough, the resident had looked straight at her, took in her mismatched, bizarre apparel, smiled and said good morning.

Good morning.

It was the worst morning in Renae's life.

She chanced a look over her shoulder at where Lucky's brows appeared to be stuck in the middle of her forehead. "Oh?"

Renae pushed her hair back from her face and looked down at the shop sweats she was wearing. "Yeah."

"Have you thought about telling Will how you feel?"

After last night, she didn't think it was necessary to say anything. "What? That I'm jealous?"

Lucky smiled. "No. That you're interested in pursuing something…more with him."

"After the resident stayed at his place last night?" Renae shook her head. "No."

"Why not?"

"Why not?" Renae practically sputtered. "Because…because he slept with her, that's why not."

"So?"

Renae stared at Lucky as if half her marbles had just rolled out onto the floor.

Lucky crossed her arms in challenge. "Ah, so it's perfectly okay for him to sleep with you while seeing Janet, but he sleeps with Janet and it's over."

Renae squelched the ridiculous urge she had to cry. Tears burned the backs of her eyelids and her face grew hot. "No, because last night…before the resident must have come over…"

"You two had sex?"

Renae nodded then shook her head. "But that's not it. What happened between Will and I…"

"What? What happened?"

"I don't know. It was just…different somehow. It wasn't only about the sex. At least not to me."

She felt Lucky's hand on her shoulder and experienced the most incredible desire to lean into her, take her up on the comfort she offered. But she couldn't, simply because she knew she was the fool. That she'd not only allowed something really awful to happen, but she'd welcomed it with both arms wide open.

Quite simply, she'd fallen in love with Will Sexton.

WILL PACED THE FLOOR of his apartment, his mind on everything but the carpet he was currently wearing down.

The last thing he'd expected when he'd opened the door at nine that morning wearing nothing but a towel after finishing a shower was Janet bringing a homemade breakfast in a wicker basket tied with little pink ribbons.

But expected or not, there she had stood in the hall, smiling up at him like he hadn't run flat-out in the other direction from her the night before.

He'd had no choice but to let her in. After five months, certainly she deserved the courtesy of an explanation.

Unfortunately having been caught off guard and standing there in nothing but a towel hadn't exactly provided the right environment for such a conversation.

As he'd watched her set his table, he'd been afraid she was going to try what she had the night before and come on to him. Thankfully when she'd moved away from the table, he'd seen it was set for one, and after sitting him down in the chair she'd given him a kiss on the top of the head and told him she had an appointment at the hospital and left.

Of course, he'd eaten the breakfast.

But he was still berating himself for not leveling with her while he'd had the chance.

Which meant he'd have to see her once more.

The thought made his stomach knot up all over again.

"Look, Janet, I don't love you," he rehearsed, wincing at the sound of the words coming out of his mouth.

Maybe the direct approach wasn't the best one. Maybe he should say something about needing a time-out. Suggest that they see other people.

But that wouldn't work, either, if only because the excuse left the door open.

And it didn't help that it would be a lie.

He stopped pacing and uttered an oath toward the ceiling. Well, he couldn't bloody well tell her that the reason he couldn't see her anymore was that he had banged his upstairs neighbor nonstop while she was away.

An upstairs neighbor he'd watched walk out of the building right behind Janet.

He recalled the expression on Renae's face as she'd glanced up at his windows this morning. She'd look upset and angry and betrayed.

And Janet had practically skipped all the way to the parking lot.

Damn it all to hell, what was he supposed to do?

His phone rang and he snatched it up.

"You rang?" Colin asked.

Will instantly relaxed. "Harry's. Now."

"I'm with a patient."

"Well then just hand them an overdose and meet me at Harry's."

Colin chuckled. "I'll meet you after the session's over in fifteen."

"Fine."

He only hoped his friend would be able to offer up some lifesaving advice. Because the way things were looking, he might end up being the one asking for an overdose if just to stop the incessant war waging in his mind.

"WHAT IN THE HELL does it all mean?" Will asked Colin an hour, two cheeseburger platters and three draught beers later.

Colin had remained quiet during most of Will's speech, occasionally asking him to clarify which event had happened with what woman every now and again. Will had hoped that the mere act of pouring it all out to his friend would prove cathartic.

Instead he felt worse than ever.

"It means you need some serious therapy," Colin said with a grin.

Will gaped at him as if his friend was offering up a tiny bandage after a shark had attacked him. Which in essence he was. "Hell of a lot of help you are."

Colin sat back and thought for a moment then said, "You didn't honestly think I was going to fix this for you with a snap of my fingers, did you?"

"Why not? You're the bleeding psychologist, remember? The one who nearly fainted—no, wait a minute, you did faint—at the sight of blood at med school and decided matters of the head were more your style?''

''You're never going to let me live that down, are you?''

''Not so long as you keep giving me asinine answers like the one you just gave me, I'm not.''

His friend sighed. ''Look, Will, I told you straight up that I didn't want anything to do with what you were about to involve yourself in. Do you recall that?''

Will muttered under his breath.

''Did you ever think to ask me why?''

He squinted at his friend. ''I think you should stop counseling others because their illnesses are beginning to affect you.''

Colin chuckled. ''Seriously, did you ever wonder why I didn't—don't—want to get involved?''

''No, I honestly can't say as I did.''

''Think about it. What advice did you offer up when Lucky first came into my life?''

Will grimaced. What did all this have to do with the price of tea in China? ''I suggested it might not be in your best interest to get involved with her.''

''And in doing so you gave me the worst advice I'd ever received in my life.''

Will sagged against the leather booth. "So you're getting revenge by not giving me any advice now."

Colin chuckled. "No, Will. I'm doing you the greatest favor of all by letting you figure this one out on your own."

16

RENAE'S NERVES were stretched to the breaking point. There was only so much one woman could take before she careened over the edge, wasn't there? Forget that she still hadn't found a replacement for Lucky, which meant she was working double-duty at Women Only. Her lunch appointment with Ginger was the following day and she was so nervous her stomach refused any food she'd tried to feed it since yesterday.

Then there was Will…

Three days since the ice-cream encounter on the counter. Two days since she'd seen the resident coming out of his condo. One day since she'd resolved to put him out of her mind altogether, although chasing him out of her heart was a little more difficult. More times than she cared to count, she'd found herself absently rubbing at the ache that resided in her chest.

Talk to him.

That was Lucky's advice.

Since he'd made no effort to talk to her, she didn't think there was anything left to talk about.

As the sun made its final journey toward the western horizon, smearing the sky with vivid purples and oranges, she parked her convertible in the complex lot and shut off the motor, which in turn switched off the radio that had been playing an old Fleetwood Mac tune. The silence pressed in around her much like the humid air, reminding her that summer was still here. She'd somehow forgotten about that. Summer. While she'd spent most of June and July hanging out at the complex pool, she hadn't even thought of swimming for almost two weeks. Her mind had been occupied with other matters that had launched her into a semitimeless state. While she was acutely aware of every second that ticked by, the passing moments seemed to hold no connection at all to the actual passage of time. So she was surprised to discover that August was quickly racing toward September and that soon autumn would be on its way.

She pushed her sunglasses back on her head, picked up the repaired belly-dancer costume and a small bag of necessities she'd bought from the drugstore then climbed out of the car. She glanced at the sky to check for rain, saw no sign, and decided to leave the top down. She didn't have to worry about anyone stealing anything. The radio was the original push-button that had come standard when the car was initially manufactured. The only items in the glove compartment were the old manuals that came with the car.

She turned toward the apartment building, her heart giving an immediate squeeze as she looked up at Will's closed vertical blinds. As soon as she got this conversation with Ginger out of the way, she should really think about moving out, getting a place of her own. While Tabitha might still need her to make the mortgage payment, she personally no longer needed the hassle that went along with the arrangement. Especially when it came to Nina.

Of course, if Will had anything to do with her need to move, she wasn't going to acknowledge it. She had enough reasons without him being a consideration.

She opened the outer building door and climbed the steps, not even pausing outside Will's door as she usually did on her way to the third floor. She shook her keys out, found her house one, then slipped it into the lock. Only it refused to turn.

She grimaced and tried again, with the same results.

That's funny....

She took the key out, checked to make sure it was the right one, then reinserted it. Nothing.

What was going on?

She switched the drugstore bag from her left hand to her right then knocked on the hard metal. It was nearly 9:00 p.m., which pretty much meant someone should be home.

Nothing.

Renae leaned her forehead against the cool metal and closed her eyes. This wasn't, couldn't, be happening.

The door across the hall opened. "A locksmith was over early this morning to change the lock."

Renae turned to take in the elderly woman who had lived in the condo across from theirs since the places had been built. While they'd traded good-mornings and holiday greetings, it wasn't often their paths crossed, and Renae was slightly surprised she was talking to her now.

"I told her the community committee would need a copy of the key for safety reasons, but she closed the door in my face."

It would probably have been a good idea if the roommates had also been provided with a copy, you know, in case they should want access to their own home.

Renae tried to make sense out of what was happening. Why would Tabitha change the locks? Hope alit in her chest. Had she finally asked Nina to move out?

"I've never liked that Nina. She's rude and obnoxious and there's something about her I don't trust.''

Renae's thoughts exactly.

''That's why I thought it was odd that she was having the locks changed.''

Renae's heart stopped. ''Nina had the locks changed?''

''Yes, missy, she did. And I feel obligated to inform you that I've already reported the incident to the community committee.''

Renae allowed her parcels to drop to the floor where she parked herself soon after. She wondered to whom she should report that she'd been locked out of her own house.

THIS WAS IT. The moment of truth.

Well, it would be, anyway, if Will could just capture Janet's attention for more than two blinks.

He shifted in the chair at the swanky Italian restaurant on the outskirts of Toledo near Sylvania and considered the woman across from him who had the menu held up in front of her face and was ordering what could possibly be everything on it. Will tugged on his tie. Not because he couldn't afford what would undoubtedly be an expensive meal, but because he'd been hoping they wouldn't be there long enough for Janet to eat it.

"And would you like to order dessert now?" the overly polite waiter asked.

Will briefly closed his eyes, sending up a prayer that she wouldn't.

She handed him her menu. "I'll wait and see then."

Thank God for small favors.

Finally he had her attention.

And he no longer wanted it.

"This was a nice surprise," she said with a soft smile. "I was beginning to think you were avoiding me."

Will nearly choked. "Avoiding you? Why ever would I want to avoid you?" He cringed. The truth, man, give her the truth. You *have* been avoiding her.

"I had lunch with Daddy today," Janet said, sipping at what would have been an excellent Chianti if only Will had been able to get anything down his throat.

"Oh?" Will experienced the overwhelming desire to smack his forehead against the table. Because right there, laid out in front of him, had been exactly the reason why he hadn't done what he was planning to do until now.

He squinted at the pretty brunette across from him. Could it be that Janet was subconsciously aware that her father and his position as head of staff at the hospital were the key to her personal future?

No. His own situation must be making him a little cynical.

As well as making him feel guilty as hell.

"Actually, Janet, regarding the avoidance thing. I think you have a good handle on the situation—" he began.

Two servers placed their salads on the table at the exact same time. Will jumped, not having seen them approach.

Janet made a ceremony out of placing her napkin in her lap. "It sounds as if what you have to say is serious," she said with a smile. "Why don't we wait until a little later? Enjoy the meal first? I'm starving."

And he was going to die if he didn't get the words out right now.

Instead he nodded, stared at the various greens on his plate that looked like weeds and reached for his wineglass. He stopped short of chugging the entire contents, thinking it not a good idea to be blotto when he had this conversation with Janet.

And he was going to have this conversation.

Simply, he could not continue the way he was, wanting one woman while officially attached to another. Especially when the one he was officially attached to seemed to have had a change of heart and was now offering her body up along with her heart.

The waiter topped off his wineglass and Will watched as finally their appetizers were brought, then the entrees. Somehow he managed to smile and nod at Janet's comments on the cuisine and at the tidbits she shared about her day, although how he managed was beyond him.

Maybe he should have taken her to someplace not quite as well known for its food. Like a burger joint. If anything, at least he wouldn't have had to wait through three courses before finally being given the go ahead.

Their plates were collected and Janet folded her hands on top of the table, her smile indicating she was ready. "Shall I order dessert now or wait?"

Will sat up straighter, the thought of sitting watching her eat another course excruciatingly torturous. "No, no. I think you should wait until I've said what I came here to say."

Color suffused her cheeks and her eyes seemed to dance in the flickering candlelight.

Will squinted at her again. He was getting the feeling she didn't have a clue what was on his mind.

But then again, how could she? She'd gone off to California expecting—reasonably, he added—to come back to a loyal and loving…boyfriend. He winced at the use of the word, but that's what he amounted to, wasn't it? He really never rated as her lover.

At any rate, Janet had no reason to believe he'd been anything but the dutiful boyfriend waiting impatiently for her return.

Instead he was impatiently waiting to end things.

"Look, Janet, what I'm trying to say is…"

He drifted off. There really was no other way to say this than to just come out and say it. But damn if he could get the words out.

"Will, I think I know what you want to say," Janet said softly.

"You do?" he stared at her hopefully.

But before he could gauge the possibility of what he wanted to say being anywhere close to what she thought he wanted to say, she was saying it.

"You want to marry me."

Will nearly fell off his chair he was so shocked by her words.

She thought he wanted to propose?

He frantically looked around the place. Most of the diners were young couples, not unlike him and Janet. The atmosphere was quiet and romantic, the tables softly lit, wine bottles chilling in silver ice buckets. Exactly the type of place a man would come to propose marriage.

Will had chosen it because it was the restaurant most central to both their condos.

"You've been so adorably nervous that I couldn't bear watching you stumble over your words one more minute," she said.

He stared at her as if she had another head growing out of her cheek.

How could she have read his intentions so incorrectly?

Because, fool, she doesn't have a clue what you're all about.

Will sat for long moments, digesting his thought along with the little food he'd eaten. Sure, his agitated state could very well have been misinterpreted as pre-proposal jitters. But coming on the heels of her trip and his ducking of her physical advances…well, was the woman completely daft in the head?

No, not daft. A little naive maybe. Trusting. But not daft. After all, he'd been the one who had played her impeccably mannered date all these months, a date whose sole intention had been to get her into the sack.

"Janet, I—"

"Will, please. Don't say anything more," she interrupted, her gaze cutting away from him as she put her hands in her lap. "While I appreciate the gesture, and I really would have liked to have seen the ring…"

Ring? She thought he had a blasted ring?

"My answer is no."

Will blinked. Then he blinked again. He felt like someone had just dumped the entire contents of an ice bucket over his person.

"No?"

Okay, so he forgot that he had never intended to propose to her and instead focused on her answer, merely because it was so shocking.

Well, that, and it began dawning on him that Janet wasn't the one who was daft, he was.

"The truth is, I've become attracted to someone else."

If Will's eyebrows had been able to fly straight off his face, they would have.

"It's actually been going on for some time now."

"You've been sleeping with someone since we've been dating?"

Oh, some ladies' man he was turning out to be. He couldn't get into her panties when all along some other man had been gaining access.

"No...no. Well, not until a week or so ago anyway."

"In L.A.?"

She nodded, refusing to meet his gaze straight-on.

Not that he could blame her. He'd been unable to look at her when he'd been about to spring news of his infidelity on her.

"But why…why did you try to seduce me the other night?'' he asked though there was no reason he needed to know the answer. He just couldn't help wondering.

"I don't know.'' She finally looked at him. "I hadn't meant to sleep with…well, the other guy. It just kind of happened. And I thought that maybe if we…''

Will couldn't help her as he was completely beyond words at that moment.

She sighed heavily. "We'd been going out for five months and I thought that if we, you and I, slept together, that everything would start making sense again.''

Will nodded, then shook his head, her logic making perfect sense yet no sense at all.

"So, you see, it isn't fair for me to accept your marriage proposal.''

Fair.

Now there was a word for you.

Fair.

A word that really hadn't played much of a role in recent events. Had it been fair when he'd felt so irresistibly attracted to Renae he'd slept with her before officially breaking things off with Janet? Was it fair that even when he realized that he felt more for Renae than desire that he'd allowed her to continue believing he'd been in it merely for the sex?

Was it fair that Janet had harbored a secret attraction for someone else then had given in to it the moment they were away from each other?

He opened his mouth to tell her they were equally guilty when she patted his hand in an almost motherly way that made him wince.

"I'm sorry to break this to you now, Will, really I am. I probably wouldn't have said anything at all except that you know the man in question."

How could he possibly know the man when she'd had an affair with him in L.A. at the medical convention?

Then it dawned on him. The other man was none other than resident Evan Hadley.

He felt like banging his forehead against the table. How had he missed it?

How? Because he'd been so obsessed with his own wicked deeds that he hadn't stopped to consider that anyone around him could be just as dirty. He realized he'd missed every last sign.

He stared at her. "What if I hadn't refused you the other night? What if I'd taken you up on your generous offer and slept with you?"

She grimaced. "I don't know. I'd like to think I would have come to my senses at the last minute...."

Well, he'd been dumb enough to ask the question.

"But if we had, I keep thinking of what a mess it would have been all around."

He glimpsed an emotion on her face that he'd grown all too familiar with over the past two weeks. Guilt.

"Well, Janet, there's something I have to tell you...."

And with that, he proceeded to do just that.

He told her that when she'd left, he'd had every intention of staying true to her. That up until that point she was what he thought he wanted. He told her about Renae, about how a one-night stand had turned into a weeklong stand. He shared that he hadn't brought her to the restaurant to propose to her, but rather to come clean.

And all the time he was explaining things, he watched as her face grew redder and redder.

He finally finished the sordid tale, hoping his story would help alleviate a little of the guilt she was feeling.

Instead she picked up her glass of red wine and tossed it into his face, then got up from the table and stalked out.

Hunh.

17

RENAE WAS RUNNING LATE for what was probably the most important lunch date of her life.

She opened the door to the bar and grill she'd agreed to meet Ginger at, feeling sweat trickle down the back of her neck and convinced she'd never draw another calm breath again.

She'd waited around outside her locked condo door for two hours last night to no avail. Neither Tabitha nor Nina had returned. And repeated calls to the condo and Tabitha's wireless phone had produced the same results. So she'd bunked with Lucky and had been up until the wee hours of the morning trying to re-create the proposal she'd put together for Ginger. A proposal that had been hidden in the back of her closet inside the locked condo.

Ginger was sitting at a back booth talking on her cell phone. Renae took the seat across from her and smiled her apologies. She picked up a menu and pretended to read it even as she covertly took in the woman who had been more of a friend to her than a boss over the past five years.

Ginger Wasserman sometimes joked that her mother had given her the proper stripper name when she was born. But it wasn't a stage she'd found herself on when she'd been a teenager but rather a street corner because, as she told it, she'd always looked younger than her age, which was bad for someone trying to look older.

Now in her fifties, the pretty brunette could easily pass for forty, her pale skin smooth, her dark eyes clear and friendly despite the rough road she had traveled down.

Renae knew it was no accident that nearly everyone associated with Women Only had had it rough growing up. Not only knew about the shadows of life but had lived in them. There was a kind of scarring that only another person who bore the same psychological scars could spot. A sisterhood that automatically drew them to those who were like them. She'd seen it in Lucky the instant their eyes had met a few months ago. And Ginger had seen it in Renae.

And that's what set them apart from the other members of the walking wounded. When Ginger had offered Renae a hand up, she'd started a chain reaction that added new links nearly every day. She had only to marvel at Lucky's work with a local runaway shelter to understand that.

Ginger ended her call then flipped her phone closed.

Renae put aside the menu she hadn't seen a word of and smiled at her. "Sorry, I'm late. The last interview ran over."

Ginger waved away her apology. "Did you hire her?"

"Unfortunately, no." She grimaced then thanked the waitress for the glass of water she placed on the table in front of her. "She couldn't work the hours we wanted."

"Sorry to hear that."

Renae was grateful that Ginger never questioned her decisions. While she might have her doubts—as she suspected she had now, likely because it was taking Renae so long to fill the position—Ginger merely smiled, reinforcing her confidence in her.

"So what is it you wanted to discuss with me?" Ginger asked.

Renae's tongue suddenly felt like it was cemented to the roof of her mouth. She almost let out a squeal of relief when the waitress came up to take their orders. They both ordered salads and before she knew it they were alone again.

"I've been waiting for the right time to talk to you about this, but somehow it never seemed to come." Renae knew she was rambling but she couldn't seem to help herself. This meant so much to her. If Ginger didn't like her proposal, if she turned her down, she didn't know what she would do.

Her rambling stopped as did her words. She was almost dizzy with nerves.

"You're not leaving Women Only, are you?" Ginger asked, concern apparent in her gaze.

Renae laughed so hard she nearly cried. Her friend's puzzled expression caught her up short. "Hardly."

"Good. Because I couldn't run Women Only without you, Renae."

She stared at Ginger. That was good, wasn't it? If Ginger really felt she was that much of an integral part of the shop, then she shouldn't mind letting her buy into it.

"I don't know if you've noticed lately, but I've been a little preoccupied," Ginger said.

Renae was surprised by the offering up of the information.

"You see, I've met someone."

Renae sat up straighter. "Really? Who, when, where?"

Ginger smiled and waved her hand, causing the thin gold bracelets she always wore to slink up her slender forearm. "That's not really important."

"Sure it is!" she disagreed. "If you're serious about this guy, then it's very important."

Ginger cleared her throat. "What I meant to say is that what is important is that he's not from here, Toledo, I mean. He lives in Arizona. And, well, that's where I've been spending a lot of my time lately."

It struck Renae as more than odd that she was just now realizing that Ginger hadn't only been pre-occupied with other matters and away from the shop, but she'd been out of town. It was kind of hard to drop by when you were ten states away.

Their salads were delivered and Renae took the opportunity to think about what Ginger had just said. She'd met a man and he lived in Arizona, and apparently it wasn't easy for him to come to Toledo, so she went to him—

Ginger sighed deeply. "You don't know what a relief it is to finally share that with somebody."

"I'm glad it was me you shared it with."

"I am, too."

Then it struck Renae. The way fate was laying the cards out in front of her like a royal flush.

She forced herself to eat at least a bit of her salad, then she pushed her plate aside, pulled her proposal out of her purse and laid it down flat on the table. "Well, then, Ginger, do I ever have the proposition for you...."

RENAE RETURNED from her lunch with Ginger feeling ten times better and ten times worse. While final details had yet to be worked out, Ginger had been intrigued by her idea, first because she felt Renae deserved the buy-in option, and second because the arrangement would free Ginger up to spend more time with her newfound love in Arizona.

Of course, now that the proposal was in and things were officially under way for her new career move, Renae wondered what she'd been thinking. She was nervous, scared and overwhelmed. But in a happy, excited way.

She'd still felt like that when she'd tried yet again to call Tabitha on her cell to tell her she'd been locked out of the condo.

Her friend had finally answered and had been genuinely appalled by the news. She'd had no idea Nina had changed the locks and they'd agreed to meet up at the condo later that day.

Over the remainder of the afternoon at Women Only, Renae had managed to get something of a grip on her nerves, but the instant she pulled into the condo complex parking lot, her heart pounded thickly in her chest. Will's SUV was nearby which meant he was home. But she reminded herself that he wasn't the reason she was there. She needed to find out what the status of her residency was. Did she still live in Tabitha's condo? Or was it long past time for her to move out?

She climbed the stairs to the third floor, wondering what she would do if Will opened up his door and addressed her. A question that went unanswered as she passed his condo without incident. She knew a sharp stab of disappointment, but raised her chin and continued up to the condo. After taking her keys out, she tried her copy one last time. It still didn't work.

So she knocked instead, moments later finding herself face-to-face with a stone-eyed Nina.

"What are you doing here?" the other woman asked coldly.

Renae raised a brow. "The last time I checked I still lived here," she said, carefully rounding the woman lest she should try to close the door on her.

"Tabitha?" she called out.

Her best friend of over a decade came out of the kitchen. "I'm glad we're all three together. Maybe we can clear up this confusion."

Confusion? Nina had changed the locks without giving her a key and just made it abundantly clear she didn't want her in the apartment anymore. Renae didn't think things could get more cut-and-dried than that.

But rather than saying so, she followed her friend into the kitchen, Nina close behind. She took a seat across from her friend while Nina, of course, took a seat closer to Tabitha.

Tabitha looked tired. More tired than Renae could remember seeing her. "It looks like there's been a misunderstanding and an apology is in order," she said. "It appears Nina lost her keys the night before last and was afraid that someone might be able to gain access to the apartment so she called in a locksmith. But before she could get you a key, we had to go meet some friends we'd arranged to hook up with."

Renae squinted at Tabitha. Certainly she wasn't trying to explain this away? Even if Renae accepted the apology and the reason for the "confusion," why hadn't Tabitha's cell phone been working last night? And why hadn't anyone picked up the phone here all night?

And, more important, why wasn't she being offered a key now?

She looked at Nina for the first time since entering the kitchen. "Then why did you just ask me what I was doing here like I was the last person you'd expect to see at the door?"

Tabitha sighed heavily. "Maybe it's because you usually get home after nine, Renae."

"Or maybe this has all been a ruse since the moment Nina moved in here," she countered.

She remembered her missing notes, her sabotaged cell phone, her missing clothing and felt a disappointment so strong that she could do little more than shrug. "You know what? I'm tired of dealing with this. I'm going to get some of my things now and I'll come back for the rest of my stuff when I find a place."

Tabitha blinked at her while Nina looked on the verge of cheering.

"But just so we don't get in each other's way, why don't you give me a new key now? I'll leave it once I've collected everything."

She looked at Tabitha who in turn looked at Nina.

"What? I didn't have time to make another copy."

Renae gave Tabitha a long, disappointed look. "That's what I thought."

As she got up and went about collecting her clothes from her room, she heard what could only be the beginning of an argument start in the kitchen. But at least she wouldn't be stuck on the steps as the two star-crossed lovers had it out.

"I'M REALLY SORRY you went through what you did tonight." Lucky placed the pillow and blanket Renae had used the night before on the couch then sat down beside her.

Renae could do little more than nod, not only numbed by the day's events, but overwhelmed by everything that had transpired over the past twelve days. Will…Tabitha…Nina…Ginger.

Lucky leaned slightly against her then drew back. "It's been quite a roller-coaster ride, huh?"

Renae hadn't missed her friend's hesitant physical reaching out then retreat. She turned her head and smiled at Lucky then leaned against her arm and stayed there. "Thank God for you."

Lucky didn't appear to know how to respond at first. Then she laughed and leaned into her as well. "You know you have a couch whenever you need one."

"I'm not, um, cramping your love life?"

Lucky's eyes twinkled. "Actually I'm going over to stay at Colin's tonight. That is if you think you can spare me."

Renae's throat tightened, so thankful for Lucky in that one moment she was incapable of speech. "Thank you."

"No need for thanks, Rea. I'm happy to help." She held out a key to her.

Renae slowly took it and sat staring at it for long minutes.

"Funny how life works out, isn't it?" she asked quietly, staring at the opposite wall of the older apartment with its airy rooms and original wood floors. "Just when you think you have everything figured out, bam, life throws a curveball at you that no one could possibly hit."

"Tell me about it." Lucky settled in a little more

comfortably. "Do you mind if I share a bit of advice with you?"

Renae looked at her. "Please do."

Lucky cleared her throat. "There are always more pitches and, unlike in baseball, in life you get to take as many swings as you want. And eventually you're going to hit that damn ball."

Renae smiled. "That's nice."

Lucky smiled back. "While the words are different, it's the same advice I received not too long ago from a very, very wise woman. Advice that helped me through one of the toughest times of my life."

Renae's eyes began welling with hot tears as she leaned her head against Lucky's shoulder. Because she knew without her friend telling her so that the woman she was referring to was her.

18

THE FOLLOWING DAY Will found himself pacing inside his apartment—again. But this time it was for a completely different reason than last time. He glanced at his watch. Half past noon. Renae would be at work....

He rubbed his forehead, just then realizing he didn't even know where she worked. Back when he'd indulged in lesbian fantasies of her with her roommate, he'd allowed himself to imagine she worked someplace seedy and sexy, what with the naughty belly-dancer costume she wore and all.

How was it that in all the times they'd slept together, that he hadn't asked her?

Well, wherever it was, he knew she didn't knock off until after nine. And he wasn't in any condition to wait that long. His mind was clogged full of things he wanted to say to her. Things he wanted to know about her. They'd been there all along, but had somehow been eclipsed by what he'd viewed as the greater problems in his life. Not the least of which was his letter of resignation on the dining-room table behind him.

After the disastrous dinner last night, he'd understood that whatever future he'd thought he had at the hospital was now at an end. The Medical College of Ohio had been after him for years to join their staff. And while they didn't pay nearly as well as the private center where he had worked for the past six years, at least he wouldn't have to sleep with the chief of staff's daughter in order to get a bloody promotion.

Of course, he hadn't begun dating Janet with any such designs. That it had worked out that way—that he'd finally gained Dr. Nealon's attention because he had been dating Janet—had been an unfortunate turn of events.

Without the promotion he was left facing an indeterminate amount of time on the night shift. And right now there was something else he'd much rather be doing with his nights.

More specifically having wicked, marvelous sex with Renae Truesdale.

The mere idea of seeing her again, having her in his bed, sent him heading toward a destination beyond his hall carpet. He hauled open the outside door, climbed the steps to the third floor, then knocked on 3B. He was about to knock again when the newer girl to the apartment—Nina, Renae had said her name was—opened up and stood staring at him.

"What do you want?"

After what Will had been through, her attitude was nothing more than a minor irritation. "I'm looking for Renae."

"She doesn't live here anymore."

Whoa. Now that was something noteworthy, not to mention shocking. "I see. And when did this… parting happen?"

"Yesterday."

She began closing the door and Will caught it with his hand. The woman looked like she would have liked nothing better than to slam his fingers in the door if she'd had the strength. "Forwarding address?"

"None."

Will pushed harder on the door to keep her from closing it in his face. "I was wondering if you might tell me where she works?"

"I don't know. Now if you don't let go of this door I'm going to call 911."

"Mmm. We wouldn't want that to happen now, would we?" Will asked. "You might actually have to answer their questions."

Nina glared at him.

Then it dawned on him. He did know where Renae worked. She worked with Lucky. That's how the two women had met. How could he have forgotten that? Colin talked about Lucky's opening a satellite shop all the time. A satellite of the original where Renae worked.

He released the door, saying, "Have a good day now, won't you?"

The door slammed so hard it shuddered on its hinges.

Will shook his head, grabbed his cell phone out of his pocket and began dialing Colin as he rushed back to his place.

"Where does Lucky work?" he asked his friend without preamble.

"Ah, I was wondering when I was going to hear from you."

"What's that supposed to mean?"

"Oh, I don't know. Just that a certain somebody has spent the last couple of nights on my girlfriend's couch. Don't tell me it took you that long to notice she was gone?"

"Okay, then, I won't."

Colin chuckled. "The name of the shop is Women Only. But which address did you want? To the shop Lucky's opening downtown? Or the original?" he asked in a way-too-innocent voice.

Will said nothing simply because what was on the tip of his tongue wasn't very nice.

His friend finally shared the address to the original location.

"But I wouldn't do anything hasty, friend. She's going through—"

Will hung up on him with nary a thank you.

Will knew where the shop was, if only because he and his college buddies—Colin included—used to frequent the nearby strip joints where they'd get nice and sloshed and empty their pockets of dollar bills every Saturday night.

It seemed ironic that he would be going to the same general location now in order to find the woman he intended to marry.

Marry...

"Now, now, not so fast, man. Get to know the woman a little better," he told himself as he hurriedly collected his wallet and his keys from his kitchen table, then left his condo. "Besides, she may not even want to see your sorry butt again much less marry you."

Marry...

Even during his five months with Janet and her repeated "I'm waiting till my wedding night" speeches, he'd never really given any serious consideration to marrying her. Sure, he'd idly thought she might make good wife material when they began going out. But at no time did he think himself incapable of living without her in his life. At no time did the mere thought of not being able to see her drive him out of his skin.

Renae…

Was it him or was the hair on his arms standing on end?

The change of temperature from the air-conditioned building to the hot outdoors, he explained away, although he fully admitted that Renae Truesdale was enough to make any man stand at attention, literally and figuratively.

Why hadn't he seen it before now? Why hadn't he understood that she offered everything and more than he would ever need in a life mate? Had he been blinded by sex? Distracted by stupid preconceptions? Occupied with the other details of his life?

He climbed into his SUV, summing up every ounce of his willpower not to flatten the gas pedal to the floor in his hurry to drive to Women Only.

Before he knew it, he was pulling into the commercial parking lot. Renae's old pink Cadillac stood out like a neon sign outside the shop. He parked in the first free spot he saw, shut off the engine…then froze, Colin's final words finally registering.

"I wouldn't do anything hasty, friend. She's going through—"

What?

Will realized he'd hung up on his friend without letting him finish his sentence.

There was movement near the shop. He watched as a young woman approached the door to Women Only, clutching her purse to her side as if her life depended on what was about to happen. Will blinked several times as he watched none other than Renae herself greet the new visitor with a welcoming smile.

His heart turned over in his chest.

He fished his cell phone out of his pocket and redialed Colin. "What were you going to say?"

"You do realize I have a life, don't you? In fact, I have an entire career. Which includes patients that don't appreciate these interruptions."

Will gestured impatiently with his free hand. "And?"

"And what I was about to say before you so rudely hung up on me is that I don't think the emotional place Renae is in at this moment is conducive to…well, whatever you have in mind."

"Go on."

"She's just made a very important career step that is causing her a great amount of stress, she's lost her home and is sleeping on Lucky's couch—"

"Then my asking her to move in with me should solve all of her problems then."

Silence.

"Great. Thanks."

"Will?"

He resisted the urge to disconnect the call but kept his hand on the door handle. "What?"

"My advice would be for you to take this slow."

"Like you took it with Lucky?"

"Lucky and I are still not married, not even engaged, even though I want both so bad it hurts."

Will found that a difficult pill to swallow.

"Am I making sense here?"

"Too much," Will grumbled.

"Slow. That's how you want to take this. You go into that shop, guns blazing, and she's liable to shoot back with ammo you're unprepared for."

Will grumbled as he rubbed the back of his neck. "Is this the way you talk to your patients? It's a wonder you even have a practice."

Colin chuckled. "That means you get my point. Good."

"Is that all?"

"Yes, I think that about covers it."

Will moved to disconnect.

"Oh, and one more thing."

Will closed his eyes and cursed.

"Good luck, buddy."

"Luck has nothing to do with it. It's all skill."

And patience.

And unfortunately he'd already demonstrated he wasn't very good with that.

"IS THAT WILL?"

Renae stopped talking to the girl she was interviewing midsentence and froze at Lucky's words. She glanced toward her friend, then followed her gaze through the shop window. Sure enough, an SUV identical to Will's was at the far end of the parking lot.

Her stomach gave a squeeze…then dropped out altogether when the SUV backed up and pulled out of the lot, instantly disappearing into the heavy traffic.

"Sorry."

Renae glared at Lucky.

"Honest mistake. The car looked just like his."

"As do about five percent of the cars in Toledo."

Lucky tried to hide her smile as she wrapped up a customer purchase.

"I said I was sorry."

"Miss Truesdale? Is everything all right?"

Renae blinked, almost having forgotten about the girl she was interviewing.

Jenny Naxos was twenty-one, more than qualified for the position with a number of retail jobs on her application, and was currently working at a mall store that sold costume jewelry.

But it was the soft look in her dark eyes that won Renae over more than anything on her application.

"Everything's fine," she said, smiling. "In fact, it's more than fine. You're hired."

She'd been talking to the girl for no more than five minutes. But that didn't matter to Renae. She'd gone on gut instinct when taking on Lucky months before. And look what had happened there.

As far as she was concerned, how you felt around a person was more important than anything else.

"What?" Jenny whispered, staring at her.

"I said you're hired. I mean, if you're still interested in the job?"

"Interested? Oh my God!"

She shocked Renae by hugging her, briefly but tightly.

Okay, Renae thought, startled off her heels. They'd have to work on the physical demonstrations. Then again, she thought with a smile, maybe not. Maybe what the shop—and she—needed was someone who not only understood how she felt, but wasn't afraid to show it.

"Welcome to the family," Lucky said to Jenny after the customer she'd helped left the store.

As Lucky and their new employee conversed, Renae felt herself drawn to the shop window and the spot where the SUV similar to Will's had been parked.

If what she'd just thought was true, what were her gut instincts when it came to Will Sexton?

Now that was something that would take a little bit of thinking.

Okay, a lot.

THE HOSPITAL'S TRAUMA center was quieter than it had been all week.

And Will was about to jump out of his skin.

It was more than just this blasted waiting stuff in connection to Renae. He'd personally taken his resignation to the chief of staff's office before clocking in and now it was merely a matter of Nealon officially accepting it and releasing him of his hospital obligations.

He shifted where he stood at the nurses' station then signed off on a resident's opinion, noticing that it was Evan Hadley's opinion he was checking.

Interesting, but he couldn't remember actually seeing the other man in the past two hours. Or the night before, for that matter. This when they were usually bumping into each other all the time as they came and went.

He handed the chart to the attending nurse then turned to take in the area, halls included. Luckily he didn't have to worry about running into Janet. Although he'd met her when she'd worked nights, she'd been transferred to days a few months ago. But Evan…

He looked into a few of the examining rooms and found Evan in the fourth, alone, making notations on a pad.

Will pushed the door open. "There you are."

Was it his imagination or had the other man jumped?

Definitely not his imagination. In fact, he was a little concerned that the young resident had just swallowed his tongue and might be in need of some medical attention himself shortly. "Will!" he fairly croaked.

Will grimaced and looked into the hall behind him. "Expecting somebody else?"

"N-no. Yes."

At his stuttering, Will had no doubt Evan had been avoiding him because of Janet.

He opened his mouth to say there was nothing to worry about, that he and Janet had parted amicably—well, as far as Will was concerned anyway—but he was suddenly struck with the most devilish desire to draw this out a little.

"So, Janet told me you two ran into each other in L.A."

Evan's eyes were as round as a nearby bedpan. "Yes, we, um, did."

In fact, Evan had told him that himself, but the

other man didn't appear to be in any condition to remember small details like that.

"And did you...enjoy each other's company?"

Evan made a small choking noise.

Will chuckled, incapable of making the poor guy suffer any longer. "Oh, forget about it, man. Janet told me what happened."

The resident gaped at him. "And you're not upset?"

Will shook his head. "No, strangely enough, I'm not. In fact, allow me to congratulate you on your great taste in women."

He extended his hand for a handshake but Evan was staring at the appendage like he didn't trust what Will's true intentions might be.

"Dr. Sexton, please report to the nurses' station. Dr. Sexton, please report to the nurses' station. Stat."

Will grimaced at the P.A. announcement as Evan finally put his hand in his and they shook.

Evan looked like he'd just been given a reprieve while strapped into the electric chair. "I can't tell you how relieved I am that you're okay with this."

"Don't mention it," Will said and sighed. "Well, duty calls. Give Janet my best, won't you?"

"Yes...sure."

Will left the examining room shaking his head.

What had the man expected him to do? Box him about the ears over a woman?

Of course had the woman been Renae...

He spotted the reason he was being summoned and stopped dead in his tracks. At the nurses' station chatting with the head nurse was none other than Janet's father, Stuart Nealon.

Crikey.

He wondered if the chief of staff would notice if he walked in the opposite direction.

"Will!" Stuart shouted a greeting.

Too late. He was in for this confrontation whether he was ready for it or not.

"I'm glad I caught you during a quiet stretch," Stuart said, meeting him halfway and pretty near knocking him over with a pat on the back. "Come with me to the staff lounge, won't you?"

"Actually I..." Will began.

Stuart looked at him, his face unreadable.

"Never mind. I guess I can spare a few minutes."

He couldn't help registering that he felt the way Evan Hadley had looked a few minutes ago.

Still looked, he corrected, as he spotted Evan exiting the examining room while they were passing. The resident immediately dropped his gaze and scurried in the opposite direction.

Will reflected that after what he'd just done to

the poor guy—making him suffer before setting things straight—that this was exactly what Will deserved.

Truth was, if Nealon wanted to put the brakes on his leaving, he could. There were eight months to go on his contract with the hospital, which meant Nealon could make him stay for at least that amount of time. Then there was the option for the hospital to keep him beyond that.

Nealon opened the door to the staff lounge and allowed Will to go in first. The three staff members currently in the room mumbled greetings then quickly left them alone.

"So…" Nealon drew out.

Will had begun sitting down at one of the tables, but halted when he noticed the other man had chosen to stand, his arms crossed in front of him.

Will gulped.

"I understand things between you and my daughter are a little rocky right now."

Oh, boy. Not exactly an auspicious beginning. "Yes, sir, they are." An image of Evan's purple face emerged in his mind and he wondered if he looked just as ridiculous. "Actually, sir, your daughter and I are no longer dating."

Nealon didn't say anything for a long moment. Merely stood there looking at him as if expecting him to continue.

Will didn't. Instead he squared his shoulders and returned the other man's stare.

To his surprise, Nealon laughed. "Not an easy man to shake up, are you, Sexton?"

Will managed to remain unblinking. "Does that surprise you?"

"Actually, no." He took a piece of folded paper out of his white physician's coat pocket and held it up. "This look familiar to you?"

"Yes, in fact it does. That would be my letter of resignation."

Stuart put it on the table between them. "I'm afraid I can't accept it."

Damn. He was going to make him honor the remaining months on his contract.

"Because I've decided to give you that promotion."

Will did blink then. "Excuse me?"

Nealon chuckled. "You seem surprised. Why? Did you think I was going to give you grief because things ended badly between you and my daughter?" He shook his head. "This is on your merit, Sexton. And like I said before, I've had my eye on you for a while."

He had? It was?

Will's grin was so wide it nearly hurt his face. He thrust his hand out and animatedly shook Nealon's. "Thank you, sir. You don't know how happy you've just made me."

Stuart chuckled again. "Oh, I don't know," he said, apparently almost losing his balance from Will's enthusiastic hand shaking. "I think I have an idea."

"Oh. Sorry." Will released him.

Stuart turned toward the door and together they walked out into the hall. "Now, about this matter with my daughter…"

Both men laughed while the remainder of the staff looked on with puzzled interest.

19

IT WAS HARD TO BELIEVE it was mid-September already. Renae pulled open the door to Women Only at a bit before 8:00 a.m. on a crisp Saturday morning, giving a brief shiver as she hurried into the shop, the clinking of metal disks accompanying her. To her surprise, Lucky had already opened up, the lights were on, and coffee was brewing. Only a week to go before her friend officially opened her own shop downtown, which meant all too soon Renae wouldn't be able to enjoy the other woman's help anymore.

She shrugged out of the jacket she'd been forced to put on over her belly-dancer costume, grimacing as she wished she had thought to get her clothes out of the community dryer at her apartment building last night. But she'd instead fallen asleep while poring over the contracts that Ginger had drawn up. One gave her an opening five percent interest in the shop, and the other allowed for her to buy another forty-six percent controlling interest over the next five years. She'd been so obsessed with the contracts not because she was afraid the legalese was in question, but because the papers represented so many of her dreams realized.

She'd been so engaged she'd woken up that morning with her cheek pressed against the top staple holding the legal documents together and she still sported a dent there. She absently rubbed at it, remembering that when she'd taken her clothes from the dryer that morning they'd been wrinkled beyond repair. In fact, she planned on washing them over completely rather than attempting to iron them.

Which left her wearing her belly-dancer costume to work yet again this morning.

Her steps faltered as she remembered that it had been in a similar situation that the flirtation between her and Will had taken a serious, more intense turn.

Will…

Not a minute ticked by that he wasn't somewhere on the fringes of her thoughts despite that it had been nearly three weeks since she'd last seen him. Through what had gone on during that time—implementing her plans for Women Only, searching for an apartment, moving into her new place, collecting her things from Tabitha's condo, even though Tabitha had since ended it with Nina after discovering she had been every bit as manipulative and psychotic as Renae had warned her—there Will was, indelibly branded into the chambers of her heart. Unforgettable. Lingering. More than just a notch in her headboard, but rather a vital part of her emotional past. Simply because he had shown her, for a brief, precious period of time, what it was like to love.

Some might call her silly. After all, their relationship had been conducted mostly in bed. But she knew her own heart. And she knew with every cell of it that, while she wasn't looking, she'd fallen in love with the infuriatingly handsome British surgeon.

She tucked her jacket behind the counter, wondering where he'd been when she'd collected her things from the condo. She'd tried to argue that she hadn't purposely scheduled her visit to the complex for the same time when they'd met up there all those times. But her attempts failed miserably if only because of the deep regret she'd felt when she'd loaded the last of her belongings into her convertible and neither him nor his SUV had been anywhere to be seen.

"Oh! I didn't hear you come in."

Renae smiled at the latest addition to the Women Only family, who'd just stepped out of the dance room. "You're here early," she said, "especially considering you weren't scheduled to come in today."

Lucky came out right after Jenny. "I called her in."

Renae was puzzled but didn't question the action. "Are the students all set?"

Lucky and Jenny shared a look then grinned at her. "All ready."

Renae squinted at them. They were acting a little strange this morning.

"Okay. Well, then, I guess I'd better get in there and start the lesson."

Lucky cleared her throat. "Yes…I guess you'd better."

As soon as Renae moved past them, her friend grabbed Jenny's arm and quickly pulled her away from the door.

What was going on? You'd think the two of them were in cahoots or some—

She stopped just inside the mirrored room with its gleaming wood floors, realizing exactly why the two women were acting the way they were. Namely because they *were* in cahoots. Because in place of her regular fifteen or so students stood one person.

And Dr. Will Sexton had never looked so good.

Renae began backing up toward the curtain.

"Oh, no, you don't," Lucky's voice came from behind her as she closed the door, a recent addition to the shop to stop the music from bothering the shop's customers.

Renae's throat grew tight as her gaze flicked everywhere and stayed nowhere. To dozens and dozens of red roses set up throughout the room. To the large red floor pillows at Will's feet that Lucky and Jenny must have taken from the other room and set up in here. To where the stereo played the same Sting CD Will had put on for her such a short time ago so she might dance for him—although if she remembered correctly, she hadn't done a whole lot of dancing.

Then, finally, with nowhere else to go, her gaze rested on Will himself.

God, but the guy was stunning. Even more gorgeous than she remembered, in his dark slacks and tan polo shirt. His light brown hair was neatly combed but it still had that tousled look that had always driven her crazy. Especially when combined with his devil-may-care grin that even now made her toes curl in her sequined sandals.

"Hi," he said, then cleared his throat.

Hi? She hadn't seen him for three long weeks and now he was standing there, the room looking like it was, and all he had to say was "hi?"

Renae suddenly felt dizzy.

"Whoa," he said, stepping forward until he was right in front of her. "I think we've discussed my incredible effect on beautiful women, but you don't have to go demonstrating it for me."

Renae couldn't help the silly smile that emerged. "Sorry. I haven't had anything to eat yet this morning and…" And the lack of food had absolutely nothing to do with her dizziness. "What are you doing here?"

Will straightened his shoulders, attempting to look affronted. "Why I've come for a belly-dancing lesson, of course."

Renae allowed her gaze to skim over his sexy frame, lingering at the width of his shoulders, the narrowness of his hips, and especially on the part of him that was even now tenting the front of his pants. "You're dressed wrong."

"Would you prefer I undress?"

He moved as if to take off his shirt and Renae quickly grasped his arm. "No, no."

She swallowed thickly. She didn't think she was up for this. What was happening? What was he really doing there? What had happened with the resident? And why did she still want him so damn badly she was trembling inside?

"Okay, so I'll remain dressed for what I have to say. That's all right. It's probably better that way, anyway, or else I might end up saying none of what it's taken me weeks to rehearse."

Renae stood frozen. "Weeks?"

He grinned. "Uh-huh."

He'd spent weeks not only thinking about her but putting together something he wanted to say to her?

She heard incidental noises coming from the other side of the door and she looked toward it, wondering if Lucky was regretting closing the thick wooden barrier because she couldn't hear what was being said.

And what was being said? What was Will trying to say? Renae couldn't seem to wrap her mind around the fact that he was there at all much less comprehend what he wanted.

"Well, then," he said, clearing his throat. "I suppose since the girls went to all the trouble, we really should do this right."

Renae drew her brows together, looking at him as if he'd gone insane. "Do what right?"

"Come...I'll show you."

He grasped her hand and Renae was helpless to do anything else but follow him, however warily, across the floor to the pillows positioned in the middle of the room.

Will dropped down to one knee in front of the pillows...and in front of her.

Renae made a strangled sound, her heart thudding so hard in her chest she was afraid it might break through her rib cage.

"Wait, wait...don't say anything yet," Will said,

frantically patting his pockets, then appearing to remember something and pulling up a corner on one of the pillows instead. Renae stared at the square ring box, the air rushing from her lungs.

She began backing away.

"Oh, no, you don't," Will said, tugging her toward him again. "You're not going anywhere until I've said what I came here to say."

"Will...I don't—"

"Shh. You don't even know what it is yet."

No...but she was getting the sneaking suspicion of what it might be. And she wasn't anywhere near—

Will popped open the box and held it up to her.

She squeezed her eyes shut without seeing the contents.

Oh God, oh God, oh God.

"Renae Elizabeth Truesdale...would you do me the honor of accompanying me home to meet my parents?"

Renae's eyes flew open. "What did you just say?" She finally registered what the box held. Rather than a diamond solitaire, she was staring at a diamond navel ring.

The unexpected gift made joy bubble inside her chest.

"May I?" Will said, taking the ring out of the box.

Renae looked at the red crystal navel ring she currently had on. "I'd like that."

After a few fumbled attempts, she decided she should let him off the hook. "Here...maybe it would be better if I do it."

She easily removed the one she had on and inserted the new one. The precious gem flashed in the warm overhead lights.

"Mmm," Will hummed, pressing his mouth against the ring and her stomach. A delicious shiver ran the length of Renae's back as she knelt down in front of him so they could be face-to-face.

"Where's home," she whispered, feeling so much love for the man in front of her that she virtually swam in it.

His gaze swept over her face as if he couldn't quite believe she was there. "London," he said. "Actually it's South London in a place called Southwark on the other side of the Thames."

"And you want me to go because..."

"I want you to meet my family. You know, my parents, my four brothers and sisters. The whole lot, in fact."

Renae blinked, so overwhelmed with his nearness that she almost couldn't concentrate on what he was saying. "And you want me to do that because..."

He looked at her as if affronted by the question. "Because I·love you, of course."

The matter-of-fact way he said the words—as if the state of his heart should have been obvious to her—made her almost burst with the urge to laugh deliriously.

And, she realized, in a twisted kind of way, she *had* known he loved her.

In her life, she had never been wanted so fully, so passionately by a man. During their short time together, he'd made her feel desired and needed in a way that at the time she had mistaken for lust. But lust didn't last.

Now, while she read physical need on Will's face, she also saw love there, shining at her, drawing her in, making her feel warm in places that had nothing to do with sex.

Then he was kissing her. And Renae was kissing him back.

Within seconds they were sprawled across the pillows in a riot of clinking disks.

His elbow caught her in the stomach when he reached for her breast.

"Ouch."

"Apologies."

She accidentally got her fingers tangled in his hair and tried pulling them free.

"Careful."

"Sorry."

Then they got it right, stroking and petting and

hungrily kissing each other as if nothing else existed in the world. And in that one moment, nothing else did.

Finally Will drew back, his breathing ragged, his blue eyes almost black with need.

"And the resident?" she asked between attempts to catch her own breath.

"The resident? Oh, Janet, you mean. History, her. The instant you came into my life. Only I didn't realize it until she came back from L.A." He drew a finger along the edge of her top, flicking a couple of the disks so that they clinked. "You seemed surprised to find a belly ring in the box," he said, his gaze lifting to her. "Were you expecting something else?"

Renae found it almost impossible to swallow when her body clamored so loudly for his. "I don't know. Was there a possibility it could have been something else?"

He gave her that lopsided grin she loved so much. Ignoring her question, he asked, "And suppose that it was—something else, I mean?"

She didn't blink as she held his gaze. "Well, then, I would have given you the only answer I could: yes."

He pulled her so close so fast they nearly fell off the pillows.

Renae gasped.

"Then we'll have to go shopping for one together in London. Harrods, maybe. Yes, very definitely Harrods." He pulled back to look at her. "Would you mind if the ceremony actually took place in Southwark? My mother would love that."

Renae twisted her lips, wondering if there was a time when she'd ever felt so complete, so happy, so incredibly aroused. "Oh, I don't know. I guess it depends."

He raised his brows. "On what?"

"On whether or not you still want me to be your wife once you find out I used to be a stripper."

He stared at her for a long, silent moment.

Then he grinned. "A stripper, huh?"

"Uh-huh. It was kind of a family trade."

He kissed her long and hard. "You realize you just gave me a great fantasy?"

She took his hand and placed it solidly between her legs. "Will, I'm giving you the whole package."

"You wicked, wicked woman you..."

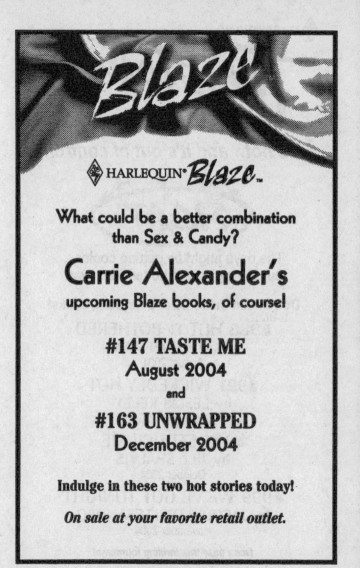

HARLEQUIN®

Temptation®

It's hot...and it's out of control!

**The days might be getting cooler...
but the nights are hotter than ever!**

Don't miss these bold, ultra-sexy books!

#988 HOT & BOTHERED
by KATE HOFFMANN
August 2004

#991 WICKEDLY HOT
by LESLIE KELLY
September 2004

#995 SEDUCE ME
by JILL SHALVIS
October 2004

#999 WE'VE GOT TONIGHT
by JACQUIE D'ALESSANDRO
November 2004

Don't miss this thrilling foursome!

www.eHarlequin.com   HTITF

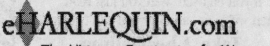

If you enjoyed what you just read,
then we've got an offer you can't resist!

Take 2 bestselling love stories FREE!

Plus get a FREE surprise gift!

On sale now

girls' night in

21 of today's hottest
female authors
1 fabulous short-story collection
And all for a good cause.

Featuring *New York Times* **bestselling authors**

Jennifer Weiner (author of *Good in Bed*),
Sophie Kinsella (author of *Confessions of a Shopaholic*),
Meg Cabot (author of *The Princess Diaries*)

Net proceeds to benefit War Child, a network of organizations
dedicated to helping children affected by war.

Also featuring bestselling authors...

Carole Matthews, Sarah Mlynowski, Isabel Wolff, Lynda Curnyn,
Chris Manby, Alisa Valdes-Rodriguez, Jill A. Davis, Megan McCafferty,
Emily Barr, Jessica Adams, Lisa Jewell, Lauren Henderson,
Stella Duffy, Jenny Colgan, Anna Maxted, Adèle Lang,
Marian Keyes and Louise Bagshawe

www.RedDressInk.com   www.WarChildusa.org

Available wherever trade paperbacks are sold.